Hadley took Mauricio's hand and led him outside.

The night air was cool, the big Texas sky dotted with a few stars and a half moon.

She heard him sigh and looked over at him.

"Changing your mind?" he asked.

"Are you?"

"Not a damned bit but I don't want this to be something I forced on you."

She turned and closed the small distance between them, putting her hand on the back of his neck as she went up on tiptoe and kissed him hard and deep.

"I'm exactly where I want to be tonight."

He lifted her off her feet and into his arms. "That's all I wanted to hear."

* * *

One Night with His Ex is the first story
in the One Night trilogy.

Dear Reader,

Have you ever noticed how falling in love isn't something we can control? When I was a girl, I used to imagine who I'd fall in love with, but the reality ended up being very different. Sometimes, I think we tell ourselves we want one thing, maybe because of who we hang out with or how we're raised, but then, one day, someone walks into our life and bam! We start falling in love.

That's how it was for Hadley and Mauricio when they met but, as the story opens, they've already decided to call it quits. Their one-night hookup is meant to be goodbye, but there is no more expectation that they have to be the perfect couple. They're both able to be themselves, which starts them down the path to falling for each other again. But, their past problems are still there and both of them have to find a way to trust each other and themselves if they are going to be happy together.

I hope you enjoy returning to Cole's Hill, Texas, and seeing some of your favorite characters, as well.

Happy reading,

Katherine Garbera

KATHERINE GARBERA

ONE NIGHT WITH HIS EX

PAPL
DISCARDED

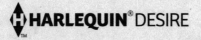

Recycling programs
for this product may
not exist in your area.

ISBN-13: 978-1-335-60395-1

One Night with His Ex

Copyright © 2019 by Katherine Garbera

Printed in U.S.A.

Katherine Garbera is the *USA TODAY* bestselling author of more than ninety-five books. Her writing is known for its emotional punch and sizzling sensuality. She lives in the Midlands of the UK with the love of her life; her son, who recently graduated university; and a spoiled miniature dachshund. You can find her online on at www.katherinegarbera.com and on Facebook, Twitter and Instagram.

Books by Katherine Garbera

Harlequin Desire

The Wild Caruthers Bachelors
Tycoon Cowboy's Baby Surprise
The Tycoon's Fiancée Deal
Craving His Best Friend's Ex

Cole's Hill Bachelors
Rancher Untamed

One Night
One Night with His Ex

Visit her Author Profile page at Harlequin.com, or katherinegarbera.com, for more titles.

You can find Katherine Garbera on Facebook, along with other Harlequin Desire authors, at Facebook.com/harlequindesireauthors.

This book is dedicated to
happy couples everywhere and to
those still searching for the one.

Acknowledgments

I know I'm always thanking the same people but, when you live in a different country than all of your friends and they are willing to video chat with you once a week, I think it deserves some thanks. Eve Gaddy and Nancy Thompson, I honestly don't know what I'd do without you both. You make me laugh, let me whine, talk plots and do sprints with me. Basically, you keep me going and I love you both!

One

Hadley Everton both loved and hated living in Cole's Hill, Texas. To be fair, the town had been growing ever since the joint NASA-SpaceNow training facility had opened on its outskirts, but those small-town minds weren't keeping up. Today, she had dodged several well-meaning society matrons from the upscale Five Families neighborhood who were all concerned about her lack of a man. Since this was her sister's engagement party, everyone in her mother's circle of friends had fixed their eyes on her as the next one to finally wise up and land herself a husband.

It wasn't as if Cole's Hill didn't have its share of eligible bachelors for her to pick from, as her parents' neighbor Mrs. Zane had pointed out with her usual blend of sweet bluntness. Hadley could choose from any of them. Though in her infinite wisdom, Mrs. Zane advised her to stay away from the Velasquez brothers, especially after her recent breakup with Mauricio.

Seeing two more of her mother's friends, Mrs. Abernathy and Mrs. Crandall, making a beeline toward her, Hadley faked a sneezing fit and ducked into the country club's kitchen. The waitstaff were busy living up to her mother's exacting standards, preparing the trays of food for circulation, so they didn't care if Hadley had broken up with her "one good prospect" and seemed doomed to a life as a single woman.

She stood in the corner near the door to be out of the way of the staff, which unfortunately left her in earshot of her busybody pursuers.

"I heard she told him if he didn't put a ring on her finger, she was out of there," Mrs. Abernathy said.

"And he just said see you later. What is wrong with young people these days? He should have asked her then and there. He's almost thirty and it's not like anyone else is going to be interested in him if he couldn't make Hadley happy," Mrs. Crandall added.

Hadley turned to leave the kitchen via the back door but bumped into someone. She glanced up with an apology on her lips, but froze when she saw it was her sister, Helena.

Helena was the pretty sister, with a heart-shaped face, naturally thick eyebrows and blue eyes that Hadley had always envied. She stood a few inches taller than Hadley, as well. Today she wore a slim-fitting sheath that showed off her curves in a subtle way. Normally, her sister was very low key and laid back, but Hadley noticed she seemed tense.

"What are you doing in here?" Hadley asked.

"Same as you," Helena said. Reaching up, she tucked a strand of Hadley's hair behind her ear where it had escaped from her low chignon.

Hadley pulled the tendril back down to frame her face. Her older sister was forever acting like Hadley was still an eight-year-old and Helena was the more sophisticated ten-year-old.

"Hardly. This is your party," Hadley said, moving away from the door and the women who were still talking about her and Mauricio.

"Girls. What are y'all doing?" their mother asked as she entered the kitchen. Candace Everton was the spitting image of Helena, just twenty-one years older. She kept the grays at bay in her natural strawberry blond hair with bi-weekly appointments at her hair salon and kept her figure by playing in a women's tennis league at the club.

Their mother had always had it all together and there were times when Hadley wished she had just a tenth of her mom's ease when it came to dealing with the social pressures of living in Cole's Hill. But she never had.

Candace inspected a tray of canapés that one of the uniformed waiters was about to take out and wrinkled her nose at him. "This looks sloppy. Please get a clean tray before you serve my guests."

The waiter turned around as their mother walked

toward them. Hadley found herself standing a little taller and tucked the tendril that Helena had been messing with earlier back behind her ear.

"Just enjoying a moment of quiet," Helena said. "I asked Hadley to help me with my zipper. It felt like the hook had come undone."

"Let me see," Mother said.

Helena turned around and their mother checked the hook and eye before wrapping her arm around both of her daughters' shoulders. "Ready to get back to the party?"

No, but clearly that wasn't the answer their mom wanted. She urged them both toward the door that led out of the kitchen.

When she got back out into the living room, Hadley came to a stop as she saw Mauricio Velasquez standing there. Of course, he looked like he'd stepped out of her hottest dreams. That was the thing no one had warned her about with breakups and broken hearts. She might be ready to move on, but her damned subconscious kept churning him up in the middle of the night and giving him a starring role in her sexiest dreams.

He had what she'd heard the old biddies in town refer to as a chiseled jaw; his neatly trimmed eyebrows framed eyes that were as black as her favorite dark chocolate. When he looked at her, she always felt like he could see straight past the layers she used to keep the world at bay to the very heart of her. But she knew that was a lie. Had he been able to do that, he wouldn't have invited Marnie Masters, the femme fatale of Cole's Hill, into his bed, while he and Hadley were taking a break in their relationship. She had believed they were going to get back together up until the moment she found out about Marnie.

"Hadley, what are you doing?" Mother said, putting her hand on Hadley's shoulder.

"Sorry, Mother, I just saw Mauricio."

"So?"

"I'm not ready to talk to him," she said.

"This is Helena's day, sweet child, so you will straighten Grandma's pearls and walk over there and greet him like he's an old friend," Mother said.

She took a deep breath and looked over at Helena. "You're right. Sorry, Hel."

She'd known he'd be here. Mauricio and her sister's fiancé were best friends and had been since high school. It wasn't as if she could ask everyone she knew to stop socializing with him. Helena had even taken her to brunch at her favorite place to break the news that Mo would be in the wedding party. The picture of him walking out of his bathroom in a towel with the town flirt Marnie Masters right behind him had flashed through Hadley's mind. But it didn't matter. She had to be there for her sister.

"It's okay," Helena said. "I did warn you he'd be here today. Malcolm asked him to be a groomsman so you're going to see him at all the pre-wedding events."

"She's got this," Mother said. "I raised you girls to have steel in your backbones. And manners."

"That's right, you did," Hadley agreed. She wished it were that easy, but when she saw Mauricio, he stirred to life so many different emotions. Anger she could understand, and sadness of course; it was hard to move on. Then there was guilt. But another feeling entirely came into play when her gaze drifted down his body, to that tailor-made suit that emphasized the width of his broad shoulders, the jacket buttoned neatly at his waist showing off the slimness of his hips, the pants displaying those long legs to perfection.

She groaned but Helena pinched her in warning. She straightened her shoulders and realized that Jackson Donovan had come in behind Mauricio. Jackson was Hadley's date for the event, and as he waved at her, Mauricio turned to greet him.

"He better not make a scene at my baby's party," Mother said.

"He won't," Hadley said with a confidence she was far from believing as she headed off to run interference between her ex-lover and her new boyfriend.

Mauricio had taken care to arrive late at the engagement party, even though Malcolm Ferris was one of his best friends. He'd known today was going to be a challenge and he'd never been one of those men who could just smile when he was pissed off. His twin brother always said it was the reason they were so good at speculative business ventures. They weren't afraid to fight for the underdog or walk into a bad situation and make the best of it. Though Mo had his doubts, Alec had found a way to make that work. For Mauricio it was real estate, for Alec it was technology and social media. Frankly, Mo didn't understand his brother's multi-million-dollar business but there was one thing he did understand... No matter how many months passed, he still couldn't look at Hadley Everton and not feel his blood start to flow heavier in his veins.

She looked like a perfect Southern lady today. Her dress was a beautiful navy blue that hugged her slim torso, drawing his eyes to her delicate neck encircled with her heirloom strand of pearls. Damn if there wasn't something sexy about seeing a lady all dressed up and knowing what she looked like naked.

He cursed and started to turn to leave the party. He wasn't going to be able to keep his cool. But just then Jackson Donovan walked up next to him. The two of them had always rubbed each other the wrong way. Ever since their school days, Jackson had been a goody-two-shoes. The only thing that had changed was that back then he had been a skinny geek and now he was six foot five and muscular.

"Mo, good to see you," Jackson said, holding out his hand.

Mo shook it, keeping his grip light, but Jackson squeezed before letting go. "I didn't know you knew Malcolm."

"I don't, well, not really. I'm here with Hadley."

Mo saw red. Sure, they were broken up and it felt final this time, but Hadley could do better than this—

"Hello, boys," Hadley said, joining the two of them. She gave Jackson a kiss on the cheek before turning to smile at Mauricio.

Mauricio took a deep breath. "Hiya, Had. You look gorgeous as usual."

"Thank you," she said, with a tiny nod. "I hope you'll excuse us, Mauricio. I promised Mother I'd bring Jackson over to meet her cousin."

"Of course."

She slipped her hand into the crook of Jackson's elbow and Mo watched her walk away, unable to tear his eyes from the curves of her hips. Had her legs always been that long?

"Mo, I was surprised to see you chatting with Jackson," his brother Diego said as he handed him a longneck Lone Star beer.

Mauricio brought the bottle to his lips and took a long pull. "Mama told me to mind my manners today. And I'm not going to give her another reason to be embarrassed after last fall."

"Glad to hear it," Diego said.

"Yeah?"

Diego nodded.

"Me too. I can't keep avoiding everyone from our life together."

"That's a good point," Diego said.

He hoped so. He was working his way back to *good*. A year ago, he'd been trying to manage his real estate business in the hill country, a reality TV show in Houston and a relationship with Hadley, who had been transferred to her company's Manhattan offices. She worked for a large design firm and was one of their top designers. He'd been barely hanging on and he'd crashed and burned, especially after what had happened with Hadley. It forced him to take stock of his life and narrow his focus to the things—people—who were really important. His family, his good friends like Malcolm and his other polo team buddies.

"Glad to hear it. Pippa's in London this week, so if you want to hang out, I'm free," Diego said. His brother was in a long-distance relationship with Pippa Hamilton Hoff. His brother's fiancée was the COO of House of Hamilton, Britain's famous jewelers, and divided her time between London and Cole's Hill.

"Sounds good. I'm actually working on a project with Homes for Everyone this week. If you have some free time, we could use another set of hands. We're putting up some framing for the walls tomorrow night." Mauricio was heavily involved in the charity, which helped low-income families who were struggling to buy their own house. Mauricio usually provided tracts of land for the different projects that Homes for Everyone were doing in their part of Texas, and occasionally even joined in on volunteer days when they actually built the homes.

"I'll be there," Diego said as he turned his attention to Helena and Malcolm.

The engaged couple were opening presents, and everyone was watching them, but Mauricio couldn't keep his eyes off Hadley. She wore her thick dark curly hair pulled back in a low bun at the back of her neck. Several strands had escaped and framed her heart-shaped face. She chewed on her lower lip as she glanced down at the notepad in her hand, jotting down the details of each of the presents that her sister opened until she'd worried all of the lipstick from her mouth. Not that she needed to put on makeup to look like a knockout.

His gaze drifted down her body to the V-neck of her dress that gave a glimpse of her cleavage. *This was a bad idea.* He should have declined when Malcolm had asked him to be a groomsman but theirs was one of Mauricio's oldest friendships.

He stood up and Diego arched one eyebrow in question. "I need some fresh air."

He didn't get far before Malcolm caught up with him. They'd met in the third grade when they'd both been dropped off by their parents on a Saturday morning for the Hill Country Junior Polo League. They'd been close ever since. Malcolm's father died when they were in high school, and Malcolm had spent more time at the Velasquez house after his mom took on more hours at work to support the family. Now Malcolm was his partner in the real estate business and together they were determined to make sure that the growth of Cole's Hill wasn't too fast so as not to damage the community they both loved.

"Hey, Mo, I need you inside for a photo of all the groomsmen," Malcolm said. "I have a surprise for y'all that I think is pretty cool."

"I think most of us are just happy to see you in love and marrying the woman of your dreams."

Malcolm shook his head. "I still can't believe Helena said yes. I'm not nearly good enough for her, but

I'm trying to make sure she'll never regret her decision."

"She's a lucky woman," Mauricio said, clapping his hand on his friend's shoulder.

"I saw you with Hadley and Jackson earlier."

"Yeah, that wasn't weird or anything," he said.

Malcolm laughed. "One of the cons to living in Cole's Hill is that it's hard to avoid past girlfriends."

"True."

"Helena already warned me I'd have to keep you in line. No fighting," Malcolm said. "Not with Hadley or Jackson or heck, even me."

"I'm not doing that anymore," he said. "That was just a bad spell."

"Glad to hear," Malcolm said. "Behind all their Southern charm, the Everton ladies aren't happy with you at all."

He didn't blame them. "I'll be on my best behavior."

"Mal, come on," Helena said. "Daddy wants to get the pictures taken so he can take off his tie."

"Coming."

Mauricio followed the engaged couple into a sitting room. There was a large picture window with a spectacular view of the hills behind the house, which were covered with bluebonnets in full bloom. Crissanne Moss, one of the newer residents of Cole's Hill, was acting as photographer today. She was engaged to Ethan Caruthers, who was related to Mauricio through marriage.

"I'm going to do a shot of the ladies first, then all of you guys and then a big group photo."

There was some grumbling especially from the men as they stood with their backs against the wall. The last time they were all together waiting like this was in high school when they'd gotten their yearbook photos taken.

He shook his head at the thought.

"I hate photos," Malcolm said. "I always look either like a creepy toothpaste ad or like I'm getting ready to be tortured."

"Just relax," Mauricio said. "Maybe look at Helena. You don't look creepy when you smile at her."

"Glad to hear it," Malcolm said sardonically.

"No problem, man."

"Guys, come on over," Crissanne said.

Mauricio walked past the bridesmaids and Hadley's floral perfume scent filled the air. He couldn't help taking a deep breath as he moved into the position that Crissanne directed him to. When she had everyone posed, she explained that they had to do a serious photo and a silly one. Mauricio realized that if he never had to be in another photo again, he'd be happy.

"Now let's mix it up," Crissanne said.

There was some jostling around Helena and Malcolm, who were in the center of the group. Crissanne kept moving the men and women to get a good balance of something that only she could see with her photographer's eye.

Mauricio stood toward the back; being six foot five, he was pretty much always in the back of any group shot. When Crissanne repositioned two of the bridesmaids, it put Hadley right in front of him.

He stood a little taller and held himself back from her.

"Okay, guys, I need you to put your hand on the shoulder of the woman in front of you," Crissanne said.

He put his hand on Hadley's shoulder. As soon as he did, a tingle went through him. He noticed goose bumps on her left arm, and she shifted under his touch. Her breath become shallower and a slight flush spread down her neck. He felt a zing of awareness go through him, and he did his best to ignore it until Hadley glanced back over her shoulder at him and their eyes met.

They both might have decided to move on, that they weren't ever getting back together, but there was an undeniable sexual energy between them now; it hadn't been extinguished. He knew better than to think that this would lead to anything more than the most exquisite sort of torture, but he couldn't help rubbing his finger over the small bit of flesh exposed by the thick strap of her dress. Her skin was softer than he remembered, and she shivered delicately under his touch.

Crissanne brought their attention back to her and snapped the photos. "Okay, you're all free to go."

Hadley bolted from under his touch and all he could do was watch her go.

Two

One touch and she was back where she'd been all those months ago. She glanced around the busy party. Jackson caught her eye and nodded toward the door leading to the parking lot. She made her way through the crowd, careful to avoid all the women who had well-intentioned advice for her, and finally stepped outside and took a deep breath. She hoped that it was just being inside in close quarters with Mo that had made her react the way she had. But the truth was, her skin still tingled from where his fingertips had been. The back of her neck was still sensitive where his breath had brushed over it.

"Hey, there. You look like the party was getting to be too much for you," Jackson said, coming up and putting his hand under her elbow.

His touch was nice. But it didn't cause a chain re-action in her body the way that one small brush of Mauricio's fingers had. That was the problem.

She looked at Jackson. He'd always been a good friend to her, starting back in high school when they'd both been in the International Baccalaureate pro-gram and study groups together. He'd been skinny and small and worn those glasses that were too big for his face. Of course, he'd changed. Matured into the kind of man she would have said was her type if not for that damned Mauricio messing with her body.

She wondered if she should just go home with Jackson and sleep with him. Maybe the fact that Mau-ricio had been her only lover was the reason why she still reacted to his touch. She toyed with the idea of sleeping with Jackson only until their eyes met. He was a good guy. He didn't deserve to be dragged into her mess with Mo.

"When you look at me like that I know this doesn't mean anything to you," he said.

The sun was shining brightly, and it was the kind of late summer afternoon where the heat was so op-pressive that being outside was a chore. She was just thinking that when she glanced past Jackson's shoul-der and saw Mo standing there on the patio outside the country club.

She shook her head. It was over between them, had been for longer than either of them wanted to admit.

"It could," she whispered to Jackson, not sure if she was talking to herself or him. "It's just…"

"I'm not Mauricio," he said with his usual bluntness. "I never will be. And I'm not about to apologize for that."

"I wouldn't ask you to, and I don't think you want to be Mauricio," she said. "I like you, Jackson."

He laced their fingers together and pulled her toward the willow tree that had been planted decades ago and now had large branches that cascaded down to the ground. He held the willow branches to the side as they stepped underneath them into the relative coolness of the shade provided by the tree. She could hear the melodic sound of the fountain in the nearby water feature.

He let her hand drop and then shook his head. "I like you too, Had, but not enough to play second fiddle to a Velasquez or any other man. There was a time when I might have considered it—"

"No, there wasn't. You've always been such a strong, confident guy. That's one of the things I've always admired about you."

"But you've admired me as a friend, right?"

"Yes. But I thought that's what you wanted from me," she said.

"It is. I mean it would be a major cosmic F you to Mauricio if you and I had clicked and ended up married," Jackson said. "But I wouldn't do anything to mess with our friendship."

"Me neither," she said, putting her hands on the sides of his face. He had a strong jaw with only a hint of five o'clock shadow. His eyes were gray, so unlike Mauricio's with their dark power. Jackson was the kind of man she'd always thought she'd fall in love with and end up marrying. But the heart didn't work that way. "I'm sorry."

"Don't be," he said, before pulling her close and bringing his mouth down on hers. He angled his head for the kiss and she closed her eyes as their lips rubbed against each other's. She opened her mouth and his tongue brushed against hers. He tasted of mint and it wasn't an unpleasant experience but...

There was no spark.

Not a single bit of attraction. There was no way she could hook up with him to get over Mo. Not when all she could think was how one single brush of Mauricio's fingers against her skin had set her on fire.

No matter how much she wanted there to be a spark with Jackson, there just wasn't.

He pulled back and shook his head. "Well, hell. I guess we are meant to just be friends."

She smiled at the way he said it. "I was hoping for something more too."

"I bet," he said. "You going back in? Want me to stay with you?"

She shook her head. She'd had enough of being the proper Southern lady her mama wanted her to be. She was done standing in the same room with a man she didn't want to lust after and pretending that she was cool with every society matron gossiping about her lack of prospects. "I'm not going back in. I think I've done my sisterly duty."

"Then I guess I'll see you around," Jackson said. As he walked away, she stood there in the shade of the willow tree and felt her hands clench into fists.

She wanted to punch something or someone… Mauricio Velasquez, who had ruined her for other men, it seemed. She felt a scream rising up in her throat and realized she needed to get out of there. Go somewhere far away from engagements, her parents and the man she was thinking way too much about.

Mauricio went straight to the bar, ignoring his brother who lifted a beer toward him. He needed the hard stuff if he was going to be able to drive the image of Hadley and Jackson holding hands out of his mind. He knew he had no claim on her, and thought he had made his peace with that until he'd touched her.

Touching her had proven that all of his growth since they'd broken up had been for nothing. The spark was still there. Maybe what they needed was one good lay to get it all out of their systems. But he somehow didn't think that Hadley was going to be too interested in that.

He ordered Jack Daniel's neat and downed it in one swallow, and then forced himself to turn and move away before he started that slide back down to the out-of-control-guy he'd been last fall.

They'd broken up when she'd moved to New York but had kept in touch with texts and video chats. Mo had missed her but he had been casually dating and hooking up as well. He'd texted her a few times saying he wanted her back in his life permanently without realizing that she was coming back to town the very weekend he'd sent his last text. Then she'd used her key to let herself in and surprise him at his place early one morning after he'd hooked up with someone else. She'd caught them together.

Until that moment he had never realized what an ass he'd been. He had wanted Hadley back but he'd also hated to be alone so he'd been playing both sides. He shouldn't have done that. He'd regretted it since then but he was too stubborn to admit that at first.

He noticed Helena watching him with one eyebrow arched. He put his hands up and walked away from the bar, but as he turned, he knew he needed to sort this out. He was in the wedding party and had to spend the next nine months with this group. Helena deserved some reassurances that he wasn't going to ruin her wedding with some sort of brawl.

He walked over to Hadley's sister. "I'm not going to F this up."

"Good," she said. "Your mom reassured my mom that you were over Hadley."

"She did?" *For fuck's sake*, he thought. His mom was going around making sure that everyone knew he'd behave? That was messed up. Like really messed up. He didn't need her doing that.

"Yup. You know what it's like living here. It doesn't matter that we're the fastest growing small town in Texas, the attitudes are slow to change," Helena said.

He sighed. "Believe me, I know. You should be in real estate if you want to see slow attitudes. No one wants to pay full market value for anything."

"I've heard you have a way of charming them into paying the going rate," Helena said.

Real estate was a nice safe topic and one that he had no problem discussing. Anything to keep from talking about Hadley.

"Your fiancé isn't that bad at it either," Mauricio said.

"Good to know…" Then after a long pause, she asked, "Has he made any investments lately…big ones?"

"Not that I know of. Why?"

"It's probably nothing," she said.

But he knew Helena. She wouldn't have brought it up if it were nothing. "Want me to talk to him about something?"

She shook her head. "I'm not even sure if there is anything to talk about. It's just he's been acting odd and we have some funds unaccounted for."

Helena was notorious among their group of friends for her tight purse strings and keeping Malcolm on a budget. Or trying. It wasn't that Mal didn't earn a decent salary, but that he tended to be frivolous and impulsive in his spending habits. And Helena was a save-for-a-rainy-day girl.

"I haven't noticed any big new toys at work, but we are playing cards tomorrow night with my brothers, so I'll see what I can find out."

"Thank you," she said. "I don't want to make a big deal out of anything, but I had to ask my parents to put a down payment on the flowers for the wedding and you know my mother. She thinks that means she's in charge of the planning now."

He did know. His parents were the same way. If they were paying, they micromanaged every detail, which was why he hesitated to ask them to invest in any of his projects. "You're welcome. It's the least I can do for causing you stress today."

"I knew you'd behave."

"Right, because of my mom."

"Nah," she said over her shoulder as she started to walk away. "Because you don't like hurting Hadley."

Of course, she'd lobbed that as a parting shot so he couldn't argue or defend himself against it. But it was the truth so who was he to argue.

He noticed Diego watching him and just shook his head. He needed to get out of here. Now. He'd done his part to support his friend and even been pretty damned polite to Hadley's new boyfriend, so he figured he could call it a day.

He left the country club and the party, but once he got outside, he didn't fancy going home to his empty penthouse apartment. He had always liked the place because Towers On The Green had been the first big development he'd done on his own in Cole's Hill. And he'd claimed the penthouse that overlooked the square for himself.

But he'd also lived there with Hadley for a short time and it had been where she'd come home from Manhattan to find another woman in his bed.

"Mo, wait up," Alec called from behind him.

He turned toward his twin and stopped. Growing up, they'd gotten into a lot of good-natured fun switching places with each other and pulling pranks on friends and their parents. But these days Alec was busy running his tech company and Mauricio didn't see him often enough.

"Thanks," Alec said. "I need a ride to the airport. Just got an email and I need to get to Los Angeles to take care of a problem."

"Sure."

"Want to come with me?" Alec asked. "A few days out of town would be nice and we could hang out. I feel like I haven't spent enough time with you lately."

He shook his head. "I can't. I have a meeting tomorrow with Homes for Everyone. It's one of my bigger projects. I agree we haven't been hanging out enough. When are you back in town?"

"Ten days," Alec said.

"For the polo match that Diego set up?"

"Yes. I can't wait. Should be a good game," Alec said.

Diego and Mauricio had been working on a new horse stable closer to town and had added a field that was big enough to host charity polo matches. Diego ran the Velasquez ranch, Arbol Verde, which had been in the family for generations.

Mo dropped his brother off at the airport and took the long way home, stopping by the old warehouse district where Hadley's loft was. He told himself he was checking out the land because it might be a good development project. But he knew a lie when he told one to himself, and as he stared up at the corner loft unit and noticed that the lights were on, he had to force himself not to call her.

* * *

Hadley spent a restless night trying to forget that one little touch from Mauricio. She went for a run and then showered and pretended that her week was starting like every other one. She had this. Of course, she'd broken up with Jackson and now had to find something to fill her hours, which made her feel exactly like the old biddies who thought she needed a man to be complete. It was just… Her sister was engaged and most of her friends were in long-term relationships, and it was hard being the third wheel all the time.

She went into her shop and took a moment to look around. The best part of coming back to Cole's Hill was opening this place. She'd always known she wanted to do something artistic as an adult. After college, her career had taken her into brand marketing and graphic design, which was challenging and rewarding but had too many restrictions. She'd quickly realized she didn't mind following a brief but hated having someone tell her exactly how to design a project.

But here at her art studio, she was finding her true calling. She still had a few clients in New York that she was working with until she could make this studio start to pay. Her sister, who was a CPA, had designed a long-term investment strategy for Hadley and so far it was going pretty well.

She had designed some lithographs of the surrounding Cole's Hill area and had a commission to do the Abernathy ranch.

The bell on the door to her shop rang and she

glanced over her shoulder to see Helena coming toward her with two thermal coffee mugs and a pastry box from the Bluebonnet Bakery. "I brought breakfast."

Hadley leaned her hip against the back counter, eyeing her sister. "What do you want?"

"What makes you think I want something?"

"It's not even nine and you're in my shop with a bribe."

"Maybe I just love my little sister," Helena said, putting the box on the counter in front of Hadley and handing her the thermal mug that was emblazoned with *#BRIDETRIBE*. She took the mug and inhaled the aroma. A skinny vanilla latte. Her sister definitely wanted something.

"You could, but I haven't known you to get out of bed this early unless you needed something," she said. Helena was famous in their family as a late sleeper and ridiculously hard to wake up under normal circumstances.

"Well, I might need your help to run interference with Mother."

Hadley took a sip of her latte and reached out to open the box. There were two cheese Danishes and a chocolate cake doughnut inside. Of course, Helena had brought her favorites so this must be serious.

"With what?" she asked.

"I had to ask Mom and Dad to put the deposit down on the flowers and now she's trying to take over. I mentioned that you were the artsy one and had already designed the flowers for the church and the reception…"

"That doesn't sound bad. I'm not sure you needed to bring the latte and the pastries to ask me to do your design. I was already planning to do it," Hadley said.

"Great. Glad to hear it. Mom is going to be over later to give you some notes on how she'd like the church to look. You will need to make some time to go and visit with the pastor, as well as with Kinley. Now that Mom is on board, we're going to have Kinley plan it."

Kinley Caruthers was a local girl who'd moved to Vegas and landed a primo job with Jaqs Veerland. *The* Jaqs Veerland, who planned weddings for A-listers and European royalty. Kinley had come back to Cole's Hill to plan former NFL bad boy Hunter Caruthers's wedding. Kinley had a complicated history with Hunter's brother Nate and after they got engaged Jaqs opened a satellite office here in town so Kinley could work in Cole's Hill.

"What?" Now the pastries were making a bit more sense.

"Sorry, sis," she said.

"There aren't enough cheese Danishes at the Bluebonnet to make this okay. Mom is going to be a complete tyrant about this," Hadley said.

"I know. I'm sorry, but I had no choice."

"Why not? I thought you'd budgeted to make sure you didn't have to ask them for any money," she said.

"I did, but something came up unexpectedly and

we didn't have enough for the deposit, so I had to ask Daddy."

"That doesn't sound like you."

She shrugged. "You know how it is with brides."

"Actually, I don't. But I do know you and you have a backup for everything," she said. She put her coffee mug on the counter and walked around to her sister. "What's going on?"

Helena chewed her lower lip and turned away from Hadley, which made her even more concerned.

"Hel, whatever it is, you can tell me," she said.

She put her arms at her sides and shrugged. "That's just it. I don't know what the problem is. Malcolm withdrew the money and I can't ask him about it without it seeming like I'm checking up on him."

"Uh, yes you can. It's your wedding fund," she said.

"I know, but I took out a large amount to buy him a wedding present and I asked him to trust me and he did...so now I have to give him the same trust," she said.

"Did he say he bought you something with it?" she asked.

"No, he just said he'd have the money back in our account soon."

"Soon? That doesn't sound like Malcolm. When did he say that?"

"Six weeks ago," Helena said.

"Uh...that doesn't sound right."

"I know. I asked Mauricio to see if he can find out what's going on," Helena said. "He was really sweet after you and Jackson left the party."

Of course he was. She'd rather he was a jerk so she could go back to hating him and forget about how sexy he was, which she hadn't been able to do since she'd left the party.

"Anyway, thanks for working with mom on this. How's things with Jackson? He's really cute. You two make a good couple."

She shook her head. "I broke up with him."

"What? Why?"

"For a reason I'm not sharing with you," she said.

"No spark?"

"Yeah," she said. She wasn't planning to elaborate or let her sister know that Mauricio was still turning her on with a barely-there touch.

"So about the money…" Hadley said.

"I'm going to see if anything else comes of it from Mauricio. Otherwise, I just don't know. Am I wrong to trust him?"

Hadley hugged her sister close. "I don't know. My track record with trusting guys isn't great. You know him the best."

"I do," Helena said, hugging her back. "You're right. He's fine. We're fine. And you're handling Mother so everything is good."

She was glad she had her sister's wedding to help design instead of focusing on her own non-existent love life. Of course, after Helena left the studio, all she could think about was that she'd said Mauricio had been sweet to her. She hated when he wasn't a total douche because it made her remember how good things had been between them.

Three

Closing a deal in Houston, picking Alec up at the airport a few days earlier than expected and then driving back to Cole's Hill hadn't been what he'd planned for Friday, but Mauricio was hopeful that after the long day he'd fall into an exhausted sleep and for once not be tormented by dreams of Hadley.

But his youngest brother, Inigo, was back in town due to some downtime on the Formula One circuit and their father was in a rare mood, treating them all to dinner at the Peace Creek Steak House. His father loved it when he had all of his sons and his only grandson to himself. To be honest Mo liked these times too. Then they'd dropped the old man and Benito off at home in the Five Families neigh-

-borhood and headed out to the Bull Pit for shots of tequila and a grudge-match pool game.

"Twins versus the baby and the favorite," Alec said, coming back to the high table with a round of Lone Star longnecks.

"Works for me," Mo said. He and Alec had been a team since the womb, and they were pretty unstoppable once they got playing.

"Or as I like to think of it, the wusses versus the awesomes."

"Awesomes? That's not even a word. No wonder you're a driver. You're not smart enough for anything else," Alec said, winking at Inigo.

"I'm plenty smart for you," Inigo said. "Who gets paid to drive fast and who has to sit in an office in front of a computer? I think we both know who's the smart one."

"Touché," Alec said, lifting his beer toward his little brother as Diego set up the balls and they tossed a coin to see who would go first.

As Mo listened to his brothers josh with each other and tossed the coin in the air, he felt a shiver go down his spine. He looked toward the jukebox and saw a pair of skintight jeans encasing an ass he'd never forget.

Hadley.

She had her hair loose, hanging over her shoulders, and was wearing a flimsy blouse and her hand-tooled leather boots. She threw her head back to laugh at something her sister said. Mo felt every part of his body tense and come alive at the same time. He could tell himself that he'd just imagined his reaction to that one touch at the engagement party, but he knew he would have been lying.

The coin fell to the floor and he cursed but didn't bend down to pick it up.

"Dude…damn. Is it too late to change teams?" Alec teased.

Mauricio gave him the finger and bent to pick up the coin. "It was heads. We go first."

"You're going to need every advantage as long as Hadley is here," Inigo said.

"Doubtful," Mauricio said. "I was distracted by something else."

"Really?" Diego asked. "What was it that caught your eye?"

His brothers were going to be asses and not leave this alone, and unless he wanted to turn a friendly Friday night into fight night and get himself kicked out of the Bull Pit again, he needed to shrug it off.

But that was his problem. He'd never been able to just shrug off anything where Hadley was concerned. He knew it and his brothers seemed to, as well. He was screwed. He'd moved on. Or had until that damned photo session. He should never have agreed to be a groomsman. Then he could have stayed away from Hadley until he found another woman. Someone who could push the last of the lingering sexual attraction he felt for her out.

"Dude, stop staring at her," Alec said.

"Shut it, Alec. I'm not looking at her."

"Whatever," Alec said. "It's your turn. Don't screw up."

He made a face at his brother and leaned over the table to line up his shot. The sound of the juke-box playing loud country music on a Friday night made it easier for him to focus on the game. He took a deep breath and broke the balls. Though he knew this was a friendly rivalry amongst his brothers, he didn't want to lose.

He took his next shot, sinking a ball in the corner pocket, and then moved on to line up his next shot. He had a pretty good run of three balls before it was Diego's turn. Mauricio went to lean against the high table next to Inigo, who was posting to one of his social media ac-counts. His youngest brother was a hot up-and-coming driver who had been on the Formula Two circuit for a few years before making it to the big leagues of For-mula One.

"Not bad, Mo. I'd hate to see what would happen if you were really concentrating."

"I am concentrating," he said.

"Sure you are. Like you didn't notice Hadley on the dance floor," Inigo said, drawing his attention to the small wooden floor set to one side of the jukebox.

He cursed under his breath as he saw her danc-ing with a group of her girlfriends, and was unable to tear his eyes away from her. He tried to remind himself that he was over her, but when she moved to the music, her arms in the air, hips swaying, his body reacted like she was still his.

Maybe one more night together was what he needed to clear her out of his system for good. Of course, Hadley deserved better than that. She deserved an apology, not because he wanted something from her but because he never should have slept with Marnie when he was still…hell, while he still liked Hadley.

If losing her had taught him anything it was that he hadn't wanted things to end so horribly between them.

He took another long swallow of his beer. That kind of thinking was dangerous, because he knew if he let himself dwell on it too long, he'd start believing that it was a viable option. That sleeping with his ex would be the solution to finally getting over her.

The music changed to a slow song—"Night Changes" by One Direction—one of her favorite songs. Mauricio watched as most of her friends left the dance floor, Hadley following behind them. Without thinking, he put his beer down and walked to the dance floor.

"Do you want to dance?" he asked. "I realize I'm not your first choice but I know you love this song. And I'm sorry."

"Sorry for what?" she asked.

"How I behaved. We never really talked about it."

"I don't want to talk tonight," she said.

"Then how about a dance?" he said.

She hesitated then put her hand in his. "One dance."

"That's all."

He pulled her into his arms and she put her hands on his waist. He told himself this was just another part of moving on but his body didn't agree.

* * *

Hadley hadn't had the best week. Her mom was an exacting perfectionist when it came to any event she was planning but the added element of it being her sister's wedding had pushed her to extremes. Hadley felt safe saying there wasn't enough tequila in Texas—maybe even the entire South—to take the edge off her nerves. But dancing with her girlfriends was helping until she saw...him.

Mauricio.

Of course, she'd noticed him when she came in. It was impossible not to when he was with his brothers. They drew the eye of every woman in the bar. Seen together, they made you wonder what kind of deal with the devil Elena Velasquez had made to get four such good-looking boys. They were the kind of eye candy that made this part of Texas famous.

Mauricio smelled good too.

She shook her head. "How've you been?"

She wanted this to feel normal. Surely, the thing with Jackson under the willow tree had been a fluke. There was no way that she still wanted Mo. Not after everything he'd done. She wanted something nice and steady like Helena and Malcolm had. But she'd always felt this heat around Mo. He made her restless like heat lightning on a summer's night. Just ready to go off without any provocation.

"Good. Busy," he said. "You?"

His voice was a low rumble but easy for her to hear despite the music. She'd always liked the way he sounded. She put her head on his shoulder for a second and closed her eyes, pretended that this wasn't the bad idea she knew it was, and then made herself stand up straight and step away from him.

"Good, Mo. Really, good," she lied, but then "fake it till you make it" had been her mom's mantra for her and her sister growing up so she figured that was okay. The song ended and she started to leave the dance floor. "Thanks for the dance."

She walked away without looking back and forced herself to put on a smile as she climbed onto the high bar stool at the table where her friends were.

"Girl, what are you thinking?" Josie asked.

"That I did it. I danced with him, played it cool and nothing happened," she said.

Zuri shook her head. "You're full of it, but we're good friends so we'll let you get away with it. Another round of shots to celebrate you keeping your cool."

Hadley drank another round with her friends and ordered nachos as they talked about the men in the bar. Manu Barrett, the former NFL defensive end who now coached football at the local high school, came over with a tray of shots for Josie. Her friend was the art teacher at the high school and Manu had been asking Josie out for the last month or so, but he was a player. Josie and Manu hit the dance floor, and Zuri and Hadley just watched their friend for a minute.

"She's smitten," Hadley said.

"Who's smitten? Remind me again why we came to the Bull Pit tonight?" Helena asked as she slid onto a bar stool next to Zuri and reached over to take one of the shots that Manu had brought.

"Josie is smitten and we are here because you set Mom on me. It's been a long-ass week," Hadley said.

"And, girl, you've been working too hard," Zuri said to Helena. "You need a night out. Where is your other half?"

"He's in Houston to close a deal. He won't be back until tomorrow, which is why I suggested book club," Helena said.

"This is better than book club because we don't all have to discuss something that we've only read the back cover of," Hadley said with a laugh.

"True. But the book I recommended is getting really good buzz over at the Paperback Reader. Teddi expressly recommended it because she thought we'd all love it," Helena said. "It's about an undercover prince."

As a CPA, Hadley's sister did the accounting for a lot of the bespoke small businesses in Cole's Hill. Teddi had been the bookworm in Helena's class in high school, so no one had been surprised when she'd opened a bookstore after college.

"I'm going to read it next week," Hadley said. She needed something to take her mind off Mauricio and a prince in disguise sounded right up her alley.

"So you and Mo?"

"There is no me and Mo, Hel," Hadley said.

"It didn't look that way when you were dancing," Zuri said.

Hadley shook her head. "You know the worst part about breaking up?"

"No, tell us," Zuri said wriggling her eyebrows at Hadley. "You're the expert."

Her friend had clearly had too much tequila, she thought as she shook her head. "I was just going to say that all the feelings don't just disappear. I mean anger should burn away all the other stuff…"

"What brought this on?" Helena asked. "Is it because things didn't work out with Jackson?"

"You let Jackson go?" Zuri asked. "I'm out of town for a few days and I missed everything. When did this happen? You two looked pretty cozy at the engagement party."

"Ugh. We were but then we decided we'd be better off as friends," Hadley said. Maybe she'd had too much tequila. She should never have brought this up.

"Friends… He friend-zoned you? Dude better check himself. It's not like we don't all remember he used to be a total nerd."

"No, it was the other way around," Hadley protested.

"He's hot now," Helena said, signaling the waiter and ordering another plate of nachos and margaritas for the four of them.

"He is," Zuri said. "I wouldn't kick him out of my bed."

"No one would," Helena added. "Except for Had."

"I didn't do that. Here comes Josie," she said. Thank God. She was tired of discussing how she let Jackson slip away and she definitely didn't want to talk about Mauricio, who was over by the pool table laughing with his brothers. She couldn't help watching him as he lined up a shot. Of course, he had to wear those skintight Levi's tonight, making matters worse.

"I think we know why it didn't work with Jackson," Zuri said.

"What?" she asked, turning back to her friends, her sister and Manu, who were all watching her stare at Mo and his brothers.

"Y'all are crazy. So, Manu, are you joining us?"

Everyone turned their attention to Manu and Josie, and Hadley forced herself to focus on the nachos and margarita, but a part of her was listening for Mauricio's laugh. Which was the last thing she needed to be doing right now. She was moving on...except now that she'd danced with him, she wasn't sure she had.

Helena smiled and laughed with her friends, and for the first time since she discovered the money missing from the wedding account felt like herself again. Her mom had told her that marriage was a million little compromises. But Helena had never really been someone who could just let things go. She was a control freak when it came to money, though she didn't know why. Their family had always had more than enough when she and Hadley were growing up.

But she'd never been someone who could waste money just because she had it and that's what this thing with Mal felt like.

"You are looking way too serious," Hadley said, handing her a shot of tequila. The nachos were long gone. Josie was on the dance floor pressed against

Manu, and Zuri had decided to see if she could tempt one of the astronaut trainees from NASA into having a bit of fun.

That left the Everton sisters, who were sitting at the table like two spinsters.

"Can't help it," she said, doing the shot and then turning the glass upside down on the tabletop.

"Don't worry, I'm handling Mom," Had said.

Helena smiled and nodded at her sister. She was the eldest and she had always taken her job as the big sister seriously. She wasn't about to cry on Hadley's shoulder because she didn't know where Malcolm was tonight or where that money had gone. She was going to keep it together, keep her smile in place and fix whatever was going on with Mal privately.

"Thanks for that," Helena said.

"Be right back. Want another shot?" Hadley asked.

"Water would be better," she said.

Hadley nodded and danced her way to the bar as Mauricio came over to the table. "Hey, Helena, I wanted to let you know that I haven't been able to get anything out of Malcolm. He's shut me down every time I tried to bring up finances."

She sighed. It figured. "Thanks for trying. Do you know where he is tonight?"

Mauricio tipped his head to the side and shook it. "No. I thought he was here with you."

"No. He texted me earlier to say he was busy," Helena said. "Do you think he's having an affair?"

Mo put his arm around her shoulders. "I can't believe he would do that. He loves you and whatever this is, it's not that."

It was somehow easier to talk to Mauricio than her sister because she knew that he wouldn't talk to anyone in her family about what was going on.

"She's taken," Hadley said, coming up and putting a large glass of water in front of Helena.

"I'm trying to reassure your sister that I'm not going to screw up things for her wedding," Mauricio said.

She didn't know what had happened, but it was obvious to Helena that there was still a spark between these two, no matter how hard they tried to move on from each other. Thinking that she was casting a pall over the evening with her Malcolm worries, she nudged Mo toward her sister. "You are going to have to dance together at the reception. Better practice."

Mauricio gave her a hard look, which surprised her. He seemed so easygoing when it came to her sister but it was clear that he wasn't as cool as he pretended to be.

"Sure. Why not?" Hadley said.

Mauricio took Hadley's hand and led her to the dance floor. She could handle herself despite what their mother thought. Helena sipped her water and turned her attention to her phone. She clicked on the friend finder app but didn't see Malcolm's icon. She was starting to worry that he was having second thoughts about getting married.

She sighed and kept refreshing the app to try to make him appear, but he was still unavailable. Waiting had never really been one of her strong suits so she finally texted him.

Where the hell are you?

She saw that the message was delivered and kept staring at the screen as if that was going to make him respond to her. But nothing.

What was going on with Malcolm? They'd always been on the same page with their relationship. She'd counted herself lucky that she'd fallen in love with a man who wanted the same things out of life that she did, but now she didn't know if she'd been fooling herself.

That's what Hadley had said about Mauricio when they'd broken up last year, that she'd fooled herself into believing he was a different man than he really was. As Helena shoved her phone into her handbag and looked up at her sister, dancing way too close to the man she'd said she was over, she realized that they all did that. Hadley was just like her, fooling herself into believing she was in control of her emotions when in reality they were all prisoners to them.

Her phone pinged and she scrambled to get it out of her purse. It was Malcolm. Finally! His phone had died and he was at home waiting for her.

Four

The Bull Pit crowd had thinned out, but Hadley and Mo still alternated between doing shots and dancing. As the night wore on, she couldn't remember why she'd been so mad at him.

When the DJ announced last call and then played Eric Church's sensual song "Like a Wrecking Ball," it seemed natural to press herself against him, her hands on his lean hips, her head on his shoulder as he held her and they swayed along to the music. She looked up at him and he was watching her.

He lowered his head but she ducked away from him.

"Not feeling it?"

"Yes and no," she said.

"Should we talk about this?"

"Yes," she said. "I know we were on a break, I mean, I get that. But why text me how much you wish I was there with you and then hook up with Marnie?"

He shook his head and stepped back. She had thought she'd dealt with everything that happened but when he'd almost kissed her, she had wanted to cry. For most of her adult life she'd believed Mo would be her man for the rest of her life and then…well, he'd hurt her more deeply than she wanted to admit.

"I don't know. I wanted you. Just you. But you weren't here and I wasn't sure you were ever coming back and I hated that feeling of wanting you and feeling…"

Vulnerable, she thought. But that didn't excuse him or take away what he'd done.

"I'm sorry. I never meant to hurt you like that. I honestly wasn't thinking about anything," he said, leaning even closer. She felt his lips brush over hers and closed her eyes. She knew that she should walk away. Sure, she'd regret this in the morning but tonight there was nowhere else she'd rather be. She'd been alone for way too long and she was horny.

For him.

This could be that farewell hookup they'd never had because of the way things had ended. Maybe then she could move on with a nice guy like Jackson or someone else.

He cupped her butt and lifted her more fully against him so his groin nestled into the notch at the top of her thighs. She parted her legs slightly, rocking against him.

He lifted his head, and she noticed his lips were wet from kissing her and his eyes were heavy-lidded. She felt the ridge of his erection against her so she knew he was as turned on as she was.

"Uh…that wasn't what I intended to do," he said, stepping back. She did the same.

"Me neither, but honestly, Mo, I think we both need it," she said. "Ever since Sunday when you put your hand on my shoulder, I've felt it."

"Me too," he said.

That was all she needed to hear. She took his hand and stopped by the deserted table where she'd left her handbag and then led him out of the Bull Pit. The night air was cool and fresh as they stepped outside. She tipped her head back and looked up at the big Texas sky dotted with a few stars and a half moon.

She heard him sigh and looked over at him.

He had his hands on his hips and his head was tipped back. The way his legs were parted, she knew he still had a hard-on, and when he glanced over at her, she saw… Well, she thought she saw him hesitate.

"Changing your mind now?" he asked.

"Are you?" she returned.

"Not a damned bit but I don't want this to be something I forced on you," he said.

She turned and closed the small distance between them, rubbing her hand over the ridge of his erection and putting her other one on the back of his neck as she went up on tiptoe and kissed him hard and deep.

"I'm exactly where I want to be tonight," she said.

He lifted her off her feet, into his arms. "That's all I wanted to hear."

She put her arm around his shoulder as he carried her toward the parking lot but she stopped him. "We can't drive."

"Uber?" she suggested.

"The only driver out this late will be someone we know," he said.

"That's true," she said. "So…"

He stopped and set her on her feet. "The Grand Hotel is only a five-minute walk."

"Perfect," she said. "It's a nice night for a walk."

"Is it?"

"I think so," she said, slipping her hand into his. She'd missed this. The way his big hand completely enfolded hers. She wasn't going to remind herself of all the reasons why she shouldn't be enjoying this. For tonight she wanted some good memories of Mo instead of the painful ones from the recent past, including their breakup and then Mauricio fighting with her date at the Bull Pit last fall.

"I thought you had book club on Friday night," he said as they walked to the hotel.

"Is there a question there?"

"Just wondering why you were at the Bull Pit instead of at Helena's place," he said as they headed down historic Main Street with its wide sidewalks to accommodate the pedestrian tourist traffic.

"We all needed a night out," she said. "You know Helena delegated the wedding flowers and interior design to me so I have to liaise with Mom on it."

"I didn't know that," he said. "She seemed pretty determined to do it herself."

"She was. She had to ask our parents to pay for some of it—" Hadley clamped her hand over her mouth. "Please forget I said that."

"It's okay, I knew about the problem. I've been trying to talk to Mal and figure out what is going on for her."

"You have?"

"Yes," he said, stopping to look at her with an arched eyebrow. "You sound surprised."

She was. "It just doesn't seem like your sort of thing."

"Why not?"

"There's nothing in it for you," she said.

"Fair enough. But there is something in it for me," he added as he started walking again. He'd dropped her hand but they were still walking side by side.

"What?"

"Your happiness," he admitted. "It's in my power to help your sister out and to figure out what's going on with Mal, and I know how much you love her so in a way I'm doing it for you."

"Why would you do that?"

"To make up for being an ass, Hadley. We both know I handled things like the hothead I am, and I regret it now," he said.

They were in front of the Grand Hotel now and he stopped to turn to face her. "Have you changed your mind?"

She shook her head. Not in the least. This right

here was the man she had fallen for. It wasn't often that Mauricio felt comfortable showing this side of himself, but she was happy he had tonight.

"I still want you," she said. "What about you?"

"I think I'd have to be dead not to want you," he admitted.

It was so quiet in the hotel bathroom except for "God Bless Texas" buzzing in her head, which was one of the songs she'd danced to earlier with Mo. He was being very cautious with her, which she appreciated. More than once he'd asked her if she was sure about this. But honestly, she wasn't sure about anything except that she wanted him and didn't want to think beyond tonight. Unlike stud muffin out there, she hadn't slept with anyone since they'd broken up a little over eighteen months ago, and though she'd never describe herself as sex crazed, she missed it. She leaned in to look at her face in the mirror.

She didn't look too bad; all the dancing had made her sweat a bit and she used a tissue to wipe at the mascara, which had left the faintest black marks under her eyes. Then she smiled at herself in the mirror and winked before turning to go back into the bedroom.

Mo had switched on the lamp atop the nightstand, turned down the bed, and was now standing at the window looking down on their once sleepy Main Street. He'd taken off his shirt and she couldn't help but let her gaze drift down his muscled back to his lean hips. His jeans were tight, showing off his physique.

She had removed her shoes earlier and the carpet was rich and soft against her feet as she approached him as quietly as she could. She wrapped her arms around his waist from the back, kissing his shoulder blade as she hugged him from behind.

He put his hands over hers where they were joined on his rock hard stomach. He lifted one of his arms and pulled her into the curve of the side of his body. "Hey, lady."

"Hey, you," she said, looking up at him, wishing more than anything that they only had this craving between them and not all of their past baggage. Shaking her head, she lifted her thigh, wrapping it around his hip. He turned and cupped her butt, lifting her off her feet so that she could grind her center against the ridge of his erection.

She tipped her head back and felt the heat of his breath moments before his lips touched her neck. He nibbled on the length of her neck and she felt a shiver run down her spine. His kiss was deep and hot and left molten lava in its path. The kind that was slowly turning her from a woman who could rationally analyze this into a creature of need. He lifted her higher in his arms, turning and moving until she felt the wall at her back. He pinned her in place with one thick thigh between her legs and she felt his hand moving up and down on her butt, his finger tracing over the seam of the jeans right there in the middle of her cheeks.

She arched against him, her head tipped back against the wall, and then she felt his mouth moving down the vee of her blouse into the valley between her breasts. Her nipples tightened as she lifted her arms up to his chest, ran her hands over his pecs, then down the center of his body. Mo had a smooth hairless chest, his skin soft over rock hard muscles that she knew he worked hard to maintain.

She ran her fingernail over his skin, and then with the pads of her other fingers felt the gooseflesh spreading out from her touch. His erection grew against her thigh as she slowly drew her hand down between their bodies, undoing the button at the top of his jeans and pushing the zipper down. She slipped her hand beneath the front of his boxer briefs, wrapping her hand around his shaft and stroking him up and down, taking care to run her finger over the tip with each stroke.

He groaned and grunted her name. "Had."

She smiled as she continued to work him with her hand, felt him getting bigger with each stroke. He tangled one hand in her hair and pulled her head back as he brought his lips down with the perfect amount of pressure on hers. His tongue thrust deep into her mouth, taking control of her and distracting her from her stroking.

His kiss left no room for anything but the aching need in her core. It was an emptiness that was begging to be filled by him. She felt his hand moving between their bodies as it dipped into the top of her blouse, his fingers seeking out her nipple through the fabric of her lacy bra.

She groaned as he stroked it until it pebbled under his fingers, and then he pinched lightly, which made her moan in pleasure and arch against him, her hand tightening on his erection.

She let go of it and reached for the hem of her blouse, pulling it up and over her head, tearing her lips from his. He reached behind her with one hand, undoing the clasp of her bra, and she shifted her shoulders so that the straps fell down her arms. Mo pulled the lacy material away from her body and tossed it aside. He backed away slightly so he could look down at her naked breasts.

Her breath was coming in faster than she would have liked, making her chest rise and fall, and the more he stared at her, the harder her nipples got. He brought his finger to her lip and she kissed it. He drew it down the center of her neck, caressing her chest and tracing the globe of her breast, drawing his finger up one side, around the areola and then back down the other side. He slowly moved his hand to her other breast and did the same thing. She moaned and felt the liquid heat between her legs. The emptiness in her center was growing with each touch of his finger. He brought his mouth back down on hers as he continued to fondle her breasts.

He reached between their bodies and undid the fastening at the top of her jeans, then shoved his hand down the back of them. She had worn a thong so his hand encountered her naked backside. His hand was large and hot as he cupped her butt cheek and lifted her so that her back arched, the tips of her breasts brushing against his chest as he ran his finger down the furrow between her cheeks. He gripped her and she moaned, stroking her hand up and down his shaft until she realized this wasn't going to be enough.

She pulled her mouth from his. "Let me take my jeans off."

"Not yet," he said, kissing her again, his tongue thrusting deep into her mouth.

She sucked on it and drew him deeper. Using the edge of her nail, she trailed her finger up the side of his cock and felt his hips jerk forward as she ran her nail delicately around the tip. She did it again and he cursed as he pulled his mouth from hers.

He stepped back and she slid down the wall as he pulled his thigh back from between her legs.

"Take 'em off," he said, his voice a low gravelly sound that turned her on even more.

She shimmied out of her jeans but they were skinny jeans and got stuck around her ankles. She finally got them off and then pushed her underwear down her legs. Mauricio took his pants off, as well.

He stood there totally naked and completely turned on, his erection standing out as if begging for her. She reached for it, took him in her hand again and this time he caught her around her waist and lifted her off her feet. She wrapped her legs around his waist as he wrapped a strand of her hair around his hand;

the other one was at the center of her back, his arm holding her up.

His chest was flush against hers and she put her hand on his shoulder as he dropped open-mouthed kisses against her jaw and then down the side of her neck. She shoved her hand into his thick black hair and held his head as his mouth moved down her neck. She felt the edge of his teeth, which made her core tighten, and she shifted so the ridge of his erection was nestled against her clit.

He moved his hips slightly and she shivered as sensations spread up through her body. She ached for him to be inside her and shifted around, trying to get him where she yearned for him. But he moved his hands down her back and slowly stepped away from her until she once again felt the carpeted floor under her feet. His mouth took hers again and then she felt one of his hands moving down her body, over her stomach, tracing her belly button and then lower, caressing her. Then he was moving his finger slowly between her lower lips, lightly rubbing against her engorged clit. She clawed at his shoulders as he pushed his fingers down until she felt the tip of his forefinger penetrating her, his thumb tapping on her clit.

Her hips moved against him, trying to take him deeper, but Mo kept his touch light and only allowed her to take the very tip of his finger. She dug her nails into his shoulders as that delicious sensation continued to build between her legs.

She thrust her hips forward, needing more, and he still wouldn't let her have what she needed. Instead he kept teasing her until she thought she was going to explode but didn't.

She took his shaft, working her hand up and down its length as she leaned up on her tiptoes, which inadvertently pushed his finger deeper into her. She smiled as she caught his earlobe between her teeth and then whispered into his ear dark sexual yearnings, telling him how good he felt inside of her and how she couldn't wait for his cock to fill her.

He cursed and shoved his finger deeper into her and she moaned in satisfaction, letting her head drop back. Her hair brushed against her shoulder blades as her orgasm started and spread out from his fingers between her legs, tightening her nipples even more and making her legs weak.

He caught her to him, held her up as his mouth came down on hers. She rode his hand until her orgasm started to die down. She was hungry for more and as he broke the kiss and looked down at her and their eyes met, she felt a wave of emotion go through her that was hard to ignore. Saying goodbye in the morning would be harder than she had expected.

She was tempted to get her clothes and walk out right now but she wasn't done with Mauricio Velasquez. Not yet. She was going to squeeze every bit out of this night they had together.

She took his hand in hers and drew him over to the bed, pushing him down on the edge. He pulled her onto his lap and she felt the tip of him at her entrance. She started to sink down on him before she realized what she was doing.

"I'm not on the Pill," she said.

"Shit," he said. He lifted her off his lap and turned away.

"Don't you have a condom?"

"I might. Let me check my wallet."

He got up and she leaned back, her body so full of sensation all she could do was watch him.

"Found one," he said, coming back.

She took the packet from him and opened it up as he came closer to her. She took her time pushing it down his length and he shuddered under her touch. She put his hands on her waist, lifting her and pushing her back on the bed before coming down between her legs. His hips nestling between hers. She felt the tip of him at her entrance as he took her wrists in one hand and stretched them over her head.

She arched her back, her nipples brushing against his chest, his hardness pushing against her center.

He pulled his hips back and then thrust deep inside her. She moaned as he pushed into her. He was always bigger than she remembered, and once he was fully seated, he pushed, giving her body a moment to adjust to his width. She tipped her head back and their eyes met.

"I've missed you," he admitted.

She bit her lip, not wanting to admit the same was true for her. She wondered if he knew that because he sighed and brought his mouth down on hers as he started thrusting in and out of her. With each thrust, she felt the tip of his cock hitting her in just the right spot. She lifted her legs up against his side and he let go of her hands to lift her leg higher on his right side, leaning more heavily onto her as he continued to thrust.

His rhythm was building and driving her higher and higher until she was out of control, making noises she only made when she was having sex with Mauricio. She wrapped her arms around his shoulders and lifted her upper body against him, tucking her face into his neck. He pulled her closer, holding her tightly to him while he drove into her again and again until her orgasm washed over her.

He continued thrusting into her a few more times and then groaned her name as he came. She felt him inside of her as he collapsed onto her, careful to keep his weight on his arms on either side of her body as he rested his forehead against hers. Their breath mingled, and she hugged him to her with her arms and legs as if she never wanted to let him go.

But he'd already let her go. She had to remember that. This was one night only. This was a chance to move on without the anger and hurt. But this was also Mo. Her first lover and her first love and that was harder to distance herself from than she'd have thought.

He rolled to his side, bringing her with him. He held her close as their breathing slowed and she rested her head on his chest, thinking how nice it was to have his arms around her. She put her thigh over his hip and found the notch between his neck and shoulder for her head. He pulled the comforter up over her, and she felt all the tension that she'd been carrying around with her for what seemed like forever melt away as she drifted off to sleep.

Five

Mauricio swept his hand idly up and down Hadley's back as she slept in his arms. It had been too long since he'd held her. He was realistic enough to realize this changed nothing between them, but he hadn't realized how much he'd missed her. How much he'd missed making love to her. While sex with other women had been satisfying, Hadley and he seemed to have a special chemistry that never failed to make him feel like he'd given her a piece of his soul.

She wasn't going to just forgive him for his behavior. Maybe if he'd apologized sooner. But it had taken him a long time to realize what he'd lost when she'd left. He'd used anger as a shield to pretend he hadn't royally screwed up.

He shifted a little, wanting to dispose of the condom before he fell asleep. He pulled away from her, felt the wetness on his shaft and looked down.

"Shit," he said, standing and pulling off the broken condom. This wasn't a good thing. They didn't need the complications of unprotected sex right now.

Hadley shifted on the bed, opening her eyes and smiling up at him with the sweetest smile he'd seen on her face in the longest time. For just a moment, the cowardly part of him didn't want to tell her about the condom. He wanted to just wash up, climb back into the bed with her and pretend that nothing had happened.

Chances were she wouldn't get pregnant from one time but he knew he owed it to her to tell her.

He wasn't sure how to say it. She was sleepy and would probably go right back to sleep... Maybe he could wait until morning.

"Mo, you okay?" she asked, lifting herself up on her elbow. The comforter he'd draped over her fell to her waist; his gaze was drawn to her breasts and he felt his cock stir for a moment. He thought about climbing back on top of her and taking her again.

"Yeah, um, Had, I don't know how to say—"

"Don't say anything. We don't need to talk at all tonight," she said. "This thing between us... I'm glad it happened tonight. I needed it and it seems like you did too."

He listened to her talking about their broken relationship with only half of his attention. He had to stop her and tell her what had happened with the damned condom, but he wasn't sure how.

"It's not that," he blurted out. "The condom broke."

"What?" She jumped out of the bed, staring down at her thighs. Her face got tight and that expression he'd come to see on her face all the time toward the end of their relationship was back. It was hard, a little bit angry, a little bit unforgiving, and he hated that.

"I don't know how it happened," he said. "I'm sorry."

"Don't be," she said, shaking her head. "This is what we get for not using our heads."

He wanted to comfort her, but when he reached for her, she shook her head. "I'll go to Pimm's Pharmacy in a week or so and get a pregnancy test—hell. No, I won't. Everyone will know if I go there." She rushed into the bathroom and shut the door.

She'd thought she'd wake up in the morning maybe feeling a little sad but this… No, she should have known better than to hook up with Mo. Things between them were always one step away from a full-on mud rodeo in the rain. Just a shit show waiting to happen. The problem as far as she could see it was that she had no willpower around him. Especially when it had been such a long dry spell…which she knew was a bad excuse.

She'd come here tonight because she missed him. There, she'd admitted it. She might not have wanted to deal with that particular truth, but she was tired of only having him in her hot sexy dreams.

There was a knock and she turned to look at the closed bathroom door. He probably wanted to get in here and wash up too. She opened the door and he stood there with a weighty look in his eyes. He put one hand on the doorjamb and the other on his chest. She saw his signet ring on his ring finger as he rubbed his hand over his chest.

"I'm sorry."

"It's not your fault. Honestly, you don't have to keep apologizing. We both came up here with our eyes open," she said.

He nodded.

She hated this. She hated the distance between them because they weren't in a relationship. No matter how much she wanted to pretend that Mauricio was just a Bull Pit hookup, she knew he wasn't.

She reached out and took his hand, threading their fingers together and squeezing before she walked by him and let him have the bathroom. They were going to have to figure something out. But it was—what the hell time was it?

She glanced at the digital clock under the TV.

Four in the morning.

Her mother had always said that nothing good happened after midnight. Of course, she was always right. Still, Hadley might not be pregnant… Maybe they could wait to find out?

She heard the toilet flush and then a few minutes later Mo came out. He hesitated, and she realized that even though she had said neither of them was to blame, she was acting like he was somehow to blame. If she hadn't been so hot for him, this wouldn't have happened, but she hadn't felt this spark with anyone else.

"Mo, it's okay. It's not like this is the first time we had the pregnancy scare," she said.

"You're right. Girl, you go to my head. Normally, this sort of thing never happens to me," he said.

"Same. I'm not going to be able to get a pregnancy test for a while, which I guess is fine since I can't take it for a week or two. I have an exhibit I'm supposed to start installing in my shop. I'm thinking I can go to one of the big box stores near Houston to get the test when I'm there next week."

He moved farther into the room and sat down next to her at the foot of the bed. He was close enough that she could feel the heat coming off his body and smell that cologne of his that she loved.

"Do you want me to go get one?" he asked. "I have a meeting with a supplier for Homes for Everyone."

She knew the charity was close to his heart. When they were still together, she'd gone with him to help build the homes and had even donated her time and artist talents doing murals in the children's rooms.

"It's okay. I think it will be better if I go and get it," she said. She didn't want him to be too involved unless…

"What are we going to do if I am pregnant?" she asked after what felt like an hour. The clock under the TV showed that only two minutes had gone by.

"We'll figure it out," he said. "I'm not the same man I was when you left me."

She nodded. She knew that. She had changed too.

For a long time, she'd been defining herself by how she was seen in town… The younger Everton sister, Mauricio's girlfriend, that arty girl who went to Manhattan… The truth was, she hadn't ever taken time to figure out who Hadley Everton really was.

And she'd been slowly figuring it out. Apparently she still had a weakness for Mauricio's dark brown eyes and square jaw.

"Want to try to sleep some more or should I walk you back to your car and take you home?" he asked, breaking into her thoughts at just the right moment.

Mauricio had taken a few minutes to get his mind together in the bathroom. While he had wanted some resolution to their relationship and the breakup, and thought Hadley needed it too, this wasn't what he'd had in mind. For one thing, he wasn't sure waiting two weeks was going to be easy for either of them. Now all he could think about was the possibility that she was pregnant with his child.

And while he'd never thought of himself as a family man, he had to admit the image of her with her belly round, expecting his child, kept dancing through his mind and making him think things that he knew weren't possible. They were nowhere near ready for anything more than a hookup.

He'd apologized and he knew it would take a lot of time for her to truly forgive him. It wouldn't surprise him if Hadley thought he hadn't changed. All those fights last fall had wisened him up. He knew that it was going to take a lot of time to show her he'd changed. And she might not…she might not want more from him. She might never be able to forgive seeing him with another woman in his bedroom.

He didn't blame her. He wasn't sure he could forgive himself for hurting her that deeply.

But he was going to let Hadley take control of this situation. Whatever he felt, he was pretty damned sure that she was probably freaking out inside. She looked so calm and almost serene sitting next to him, but she kept tapping her left foot really fast and then she'd realize she was doing it and stop for a minute.

"Whatever you want to do is fine with me. I would like to come over when you take the test," he said.

"Of course," she said, then looked around the room. "I don't think I can sleep anymore tonight. Do you mind taking me home? I caught a ride with Zuri last night."

"Not at all. Do you want to wait here and I'll go get my car and pick you up?" he suggested.

"Yeah, that sounds good," she said. "I didn't drive tonight."

He put his shirt back on; it smelled like smoke and whiskey and the faintest trace of Hadley's body spray. He buttoned it up quickly, then stomped his feet into his boots. "I'll text you when I'm out front."

She just nodded and he got up and let himself out of the room. He'd had one-night stands in the past and yet he'd never felt like this. It wasn't exactly a nice feeling; he couldn't define it, didn't really want to. He wanted to get to his car, drop her off and then go home where he could try to figure this out.

One thought that plagued him as he walked toward the Bull Pit parking lot was how he always managed to screw things up with Hadley. Even in the beginning when they'd first started dating, he'd been trying so hard to make things perfect for her. It hadn't helped that she had certain expectations for the men she dated. She told him that on their first date. It had been kind of cute and he hadn't really paid attention to it until he'd hurt her the first time. Then he realized that she'd invested a lot in him as her boyfriend.

That pressure had made it harder for him to live up to her expectations and eventually he'd started to resent her. But that was on him. He'd always been the hothead. It had set him apart from his family, even his twin, since he was a kid. People who struggled to tell Alec and him apart based on their appearance could always tell in a fight.

There were only five cars left in the parking lot. He unlocked his car and drove on autopilot back to the Grand Hotel. He noticed that the streets were starting to get busy; it was nearly 5:00 a.m. and the commuters who drove to Houston were already getting a head start to beat the traffic. Then he saw a familiar Cadillac CTS turn onto Main Street from the Five Families area and cursed. His mother.

She was one of the morning news anchors for a local Houston affiliate. She did a double take as he drove by. He didn't want to stop at the hotel, which would just raise more questions from her, so he drove past it, down toward the apartment towers where he had his penthouse, waited ten minutes and then went back to the Grand Hotel, staying vigilant along the way for his mom.

He pulled around back in the guest parking lot and then texted Hadley his location. He was sweating and felt like he was sixteen years old instead of thirty. But he didn't want his mom to know anything. She had been upset when he'd broken things off with Hadley the first time; he knew that tonight wasn't about them getting back together, and he didn't want to have to explain that to his mom.

As much as he hoped that everything would sort of go back to the way it used to be, he knew those days were over. Hadley wasn't going to start trusting him again. Not this quickly. He knew he was going to have to show he'd changed.

That scared him. He had never wanted to need her more than she needed him.

When he saw Hadley come out of the hotel and walk to the car, he hopped out to open the door for her.

"That took longer than I thought it would," she said. "You okay to drive?"

"Yes… I passed my mom when I was coming back to pick you up and so I had to pretend to be driving to my place in case—"

"You don't have to explain. The less our moms know about this the better," Hadley said.

"Agreed," he said, then drove her home to her loft on the outskirts of Cole's Hill. He parked near the entrance to her shop, which was housed underneath her loft. She made no move to get out of the car and he turned toward her.

"I don't have any regrets," he said. "Well, maybe the condom breaking but otherwise I'm good."

Hadley nodded. "Me neither."

She leaned over and kissed his cheek, and then let herself out of the car. "I'll text you when I have the test and we can get together when I take it."

"I'll take you to dinner afterward," he said.

"You don't have to," she said, and he felt her pulling away even then.

"I know. But either way I bet we'll want to talk about it," he said.

She nodded and then turned away. He watched until she entered the building and then waited until he saw the lights come on in her loft. He hated leaving, felt like he should have tried harder to stay with her, but he knew that he wasn't in the right headspace to figure out anything right now.

Six

The coffee shop on Main Street was busy with the bloggers, would-be writers and freelancers who didn't have an office to take meetings. Mauricio hardly spared them a glance as he got in line behind someone he didn't recognize. As much as he professed to dislike small town living, there was something about knowing everyone in town that he liked. Then he heard the door open behind him and he immediately smelled gardenias.

Hadley's scent.

He glanced over his shoulder, removing his sunglasses, and their eyes met. She looked tired this morning. Of course, he had to acknowledge she also looked good. But he wondered if she'd slept as poorly as he had. Haunted by dreams of a "maybe baby" and how that would link their lives together.

"Morning, Hadley," he said.

"Mo," she replied, stepping up behind him, and his body reacted. His blood flowing heavier in his veins, he stood a little taller and tightened his muscles before he realized what he was doing.

Preening in front of Hadley had never been enough to make amends for his screw-ups. And as far as last night went, he had a hard time in the cold light of day thinking it had been anything other than that. What had he been thinking?

He'd just started to get over her—*yeah, right*, his subconscious jeered. But he'd been trying.

"Stop staring at me like that," she said under her breath. "The biddies are about to come in and have their book club discussion. I don't want to give them more reason to talk about us."

"Darling, they don't need me looking at you to do that," he said.

The bell jingled again and Loretta, Alec's assistant, walked in. "You two! Makes me happy to see you together again."

"Uh, what?"

"It's all anyone is talking about this morning. Last night at the Bull Pit you were all over each other."

"It wasn't what it looked like," Hadley said. Her expression had completely shut down.

"Really? Even Alec didn't deny it this morning. He actually smiled before he realized I had forgotten to get the coffee," Loretta said.

"Alec is mistaken," Mauricio said, realizing that Hadley didn't want anyone to know about last night. He would follow her lead no matter how much he didn't want to hide anything about the two of them. "It was just two friends hanging out. Nothing more."

Nothing more. The words stuck in the back of his throat and he wondered when he'd become so adept at lying. But then Loretta tipped her head to the side and shook it.

"Whatever y'all say."

"I think they're ready for your order, Mo," Hadley said, giving him a small smile. "I'll have a skinny latte and grab us a table at the back."

Us?

He didn't question it, just placed their orders and then waited for them, aware of the eyes of Cole's Hill on Hadley and him. Even the guy he hadn't recognized earlier seemed unable to tear his gaze away from her, though to be fair it could have been because of Hadley's good looks and not the gossip.

She wore a pair of pale pink trousers that tapered to show off her slim ankles and a sleeveless white top with black polka dots. Her hair was pulled up in a ponytail that emphasized her high cheekbones and heart-shaped face. He couldn't tear his eyes away.

Yeah, he'd really been almost over her.

The barista called his name and he grabbed the ceramic mugs with the Main Street Coffee shop logo. He moved through the tables, dodging toddlers who were playing a game of tag while their tired moms sipped coffee and chatted.

He finally got to the back and took a seat across from Hadley.

"So, that was…"

"Predictable," she finished. "I'm in town to talk to Kinley over at the bridal studio but ducked in here to avoid my mom. I saw her going into the bank, but this is almost as bad. What are we going to do?"

"Fake date," he said. "We should at least seem like a couple until we find out…what's going on." He knew it wasn't an ideal situation but the way she'd reacted to Loretta asking if they were together again had made him realize how hard it would be to win her back. And they were in a situation thanks to last night.

"Fake date?" she asked and then gave him a look that told him he was an idiot.

"Well, I'd love to really date you, Had, but you've been pretty clear every time but last night when you were full of tequila that you're over me," he said. Then realized he was being an ass. "Sorry. I shouldn't have said that."

"No, you're right. That is what I said," she admitted. "But maybe the tequila made me realize that I'm not over you."

"Don't," he said.

She quirked one eyebrow at him.

"I know I'm the insensitive, macho jackass but the truth is, getting over you was harder for me than I thought it would be."

She reached over and put her hand over the fist he hadn't realized he'd clenched. She rubbed her finger over his knuckles and a shiver went straight to his groin, making him shift his legs under the table.

"You're not a jackass all the time."

Their eyes met and for the first time since she'd walked out of his bedroom eighteen long months ago, with the possible exception of last night, he saw something other than anger in her eyes.

"Let's take this slow," he said. "Dinner tonight?"

She nodded. "Okay."

"Well, this is something I wouldn't have believed if I hadn't seen it for myself," Candace Everton said as she stopped next to their table.

"Mother," Hadley said, drawing her hand back from his and sitting up straighter. He saw her lace her fingers together and knew from the past that she was fighting the urge to tuck that one tendril of hair that never stayed in place back behind her ear.

"Ma'am," Mauricio said, standing. "I have to get back to work. But I'll see you for dinner tonight, Hadley."

She just nodded. "Peace Creek Steak House at eight. See you then."

Of course, she'd pick the most expensive place in town. But he didn't mind. He nodded at her and her mom and walked out of the coffee shop. If they were going to fake date, why not live it up?

Hadley wished she could just as easily escape her mother, but Candace sat down in Mauricio's vacated seat, waving over one of the coffee shop staff to clear away his mug and order herself a skinny mocha.

"Ma'am, I think you have to order it yourself at the counter," the teenage boy said.

"Son," Candace said with the sweetest smile she had, and Hadley hid her own smirk behind her hand. "I will more than make it worth your while to get my mocha and bring it to me. Don't I know your mama?"

"Yes, ma'am, Mrs. Everton," he said. "I'm Tommy Dunwoody."

"I thought I recognized that handsome face," she said. "I knew I could count on a Dunwoody man to do the right thing."

Tommy blushed and then nodded and turned away.

"Mother, you are something else," Hadley said as she took a sip of her now cold skinny latte. There were times when she missed the taste of real cane sugar in her coffee, but she didn't like to exercise so it was worth the sacrifice to keep her weight under control.

"I am, aren't I?" she said with a kind laugh. "Now we're going to talk about Helena's wedding, but first I have to ask… Do you know what you're doing with that Velasquez boy?"

No. She had no clue. She was dating or fake dating him until she found out if she was pregnant and she had the feeling that it wasn't going to be as easy to walk away from Mo this time as it had been before.

"Of course, Mother. I have him exactly where I want him," she said. Lying to her mom about her personal life was an old habit, one she wasn't about to break right now in the middle of the coffee shop by divulging she might have gotten pregnant last night.

"Where you want him? That's not how relation-ships work," Candace said.

"Mom, please. It's Mo. You know how complicated it is. We have history and chemistry and I'm just try-ing not to make another mistake."

"Okay, Had. I won't pry, but I'm here if you need to talk," Candace said, taking a twenty-dollar bill from her wallet as Tommy walked back over with her mocha.

"Thank you, Tommy," she said, handing it to him.

"I'll get your change," he said.

"No need, son. Tell your mama I said hello and she's doing a good job raising her boys."

"Thank you, ma'am." He nodded and moved away.

"Now about Helena's cake. I saw the sketches you did. Hon, you really do have a lot of talent," Candace said. "I loved them. But we have to make sure we get Tilly at the bakery to work on this. Her assistants are competent, but they won't be able to do justice to your design."

"I'm sure whomever they give us will be fine," Hadley said. "Besides, isn't that up to Kinley to take care of?"

"I'm sorry?"

"Mother, don't do that. You know what I said—" she began.

Her mom shook her head. "I'm pretty sure I heard you suggest that I leave the details of my eldest daugh-ter's wedding to someone else."

"It's not like Kinley doesn't know what she's doing,"

Hadley said. "She's planned plenty of weddings for A-listers."

"She's good, I'll give her that. But we know what we want. Maybe I'll go over to the bakery and chat with Tilly. Her daddy and I went to cotillion together," Candace said.

Her mother had notes about the flower arrangements that Hadley had designed and some suggestions for the bridal bouquet and the bridesmaids', as well. She gave her very detailed notes to pass on to Kinley. When she was done, she kissed Hadley on the cheek and left the coffee shop, stopping along the way to greet someone at almost every table. Hadley finished her drink a few minutes later and followed.

When she got to the door, she ran into Bianca Velasquez-Caruthers, Mo's sister and Derek Caruthers's wife, a preeminent heart surgeon in Cole's Hill. She'd been in Helena's class at the Five Families elementary school but had left Cole's Hill during high school to go to New York and become a model.

They'd reconnected in New York at Sera Samson's book launch. Sera was a lifestyle guru who had launched her tell-all book about life in the fast lane with her fiancé, Lorenzo Romano, a three time Formula One World Champion. It had been nice to see a friendly face from her hometown at the crowded cocktail party. Bianca knew Sera's fiancé from her days as the wife of the late Formula One Driver Jose Ruiz.

"Hi, Hadley," she said, holding the door for her to exit. "I bet your ears are buzzing this morning."

She shook her head. "You have no idea."

"You've got my sympathy, girl. You and Mo were all any of the moms at drop-off wanted to talk to me about."

She wrinkled her nose. "School moms? Really? I thought the gossip was confined to the old biddy book club meeting here this morning."

"Sadly, no," Bianca said.

Hadley sighed, stepping out of the way of customers trying to get into the coffee shop.

Bianca followed her away from the entrance. "Where are you heading?"

"To see Kinley," she said.

"Nothing like planning someone else's wedding when your own love life is all anyone in town can talk about, right?"

"Exactly, but I've got this. It's not like I didn't know what I was getting into when I started dancing with your brother last night," she said, finally admitting out loud what she'd been thinking all day.

"Why did you?"

"Sometimes even I can't resist him," she admitted. "Don't tell him that though."

"I wouldn't dream of it. He already thinks he's God's gift…though to be fair that's probably my mother's fault. She did tell those boys they were the best thing in town every day when we were growing up."

Of course she had.

Hadley said goodbye to Bianca and tried to focus

on Helena so she wouldn't obsess about her upcoming date with Mo for the rest of the day.

Malcolm was already at work when Mauricio walked into the office. He nodded to his friend, who looked the worse for wear. He remembered what Helena had said last night and, though he had a strict rule not to mess around in other couples' business, he felt like Malcolm was dealing with something and wanted to see if he could help.

"Mal, you got a minute?" he asked.

"Sure, what's up?" he said, leaving his desk in the open plan area and coming over to Mo.

"Um, let's talk in my office," Mauricio said, leading the way toward his corner office. As a partner in the business, Malcolm had his own office but he liked being on the floor with the new guys. He said it kept him hungry to keep achieving.

But last month's numbers were in and Mal wasn't up to his usual standards. Mauricio needed to find out what was going on.

They entered his office and Malcolm walked over to the plate glass windows that offered a view of the square where the town held all of its major celebrations. His friend put his hand on the glass and leaned forward before cursing and turning away.

"What's going on with you?" Mo asked.

"Huh?"

"Listen, I'm not one to meddle but your numbers are down from last month, Helena is worried about you and, to be honest, you look like shit this morning," Mo said.

Malcolm cursed and shoved his hand through his hair, which explained why he looked so unkempt. "Hell. I don't know. It started with one deal that was sort of wonky."

"Wonky how?"

"Just the financing looked a bit odd to me and when I dug deeper I still couldn't find anything solid, but there was something that didn't feel right," Malcolm said.

"Bullshit."

"What?"

"I know you. You're solid when it comes to financing. So what's really going on?" Mauricio asked, leaning one hip against the side of his desk. He had worked hard to open his real estate business and to make it into the profitable company it was today. They were the best that this part of Texas had to offer and no one who worked here was taking any wonky financing deals.

"Fine. I bet too much on my fantasy football league. My team isn't doing that great and so last week I took a blind and lost," Malcolm said.

"Do you need me to cover you?" Mauricio offered.

"No, I got it," he said. "I've been trying to earn back what I lost but the harder I push here the more the clients feel it. It's like they know I'm desperate instead of just hungry for their business, you know?"

"I do know. How about this? I'll go with you to

your next meeting and we'll close the deal together," Mo said. "You'll get back on top."

"Great," he said.

"Who are we waiting on?"

"The Tressor Group. They're the plastics manufacturers from Plano. They really want to be closer to Galveston and the port and I have them interested in the old Porter Warehouses."

"Damn, you're good. We haven't been able to get anyone near there in years," Mauricio said. It was a listing that he'd taken since old man Porter and his father were friends. They'd both come up together in school. But the property wasn't close enough to town to be part of the revitalized district. He'd tried to convince NASA to use it but they didn't need storage facilities in Cole's Hill when they had everything they needed in Houston at the Johnson Space Center.

"I haven't been able to convince them after the initial meeting. They're coming back today for lunch and then we're going to tour the location one more time," Malcolm said.

"I'll meet you after lunch. We can close it together. Just turn on your usual Southern charm and don't mention the property during the meal, okay?"

Mal nodded. "Thanks, Mo. I know Helena spoke to you but I've got this under control."

"I know you do. You always come out on top."

Malcom nodded his head a bunch of times. "That's right, I do."

Damn. He'd never have thought that Malcolm would be this insecure, but he realized how falling in love changed people. There wasn't a man he knew who was better than Mal. He was one of the solid ones.

He let himself out of the office and Mauricio went to his desk, making a reservation at the Peace Creek Steak House for dinner and then ordering a bouquet of peonies to be sent to Hadley. He didn't want tonight to feel like they were just marking time until she took the pregnancy test. He wanted it to be…well, maybe the start of rebuilding something.

He messaged his assistant and asked her to notify him when Malcolm left the offices. In a way it was good that he had his friend to distract him from the fact that he was going on a date with Hadley tonight. It felt like it had been too long since he'd had something like that to look forward to.

But what if he ended up screwing it up? Doing something stupid like Malcolm had done?

After she'd left him, he'd been angry and out of control. This felt better. Right, even. Like he was in a place to actually be the man she needed him to be this time. Or rather the man he wanted to be.

His assistant pinged him when Malcom left and Mo went out to talk to the guys he knew who were in the office fantasy football league. They all posted their teams each week and bet against each other.

Todd, Alan and Rob were all in the kitchen having their mid-morning coffee break.

"Hiya, boss man, you want a coffee?" Todd asked.

"Nah, I'm good for now. I wanted to find out how the football thing is going," he said.

"Good. Our office is out ahead of everyone else in the league. Your boy, Malcolm, has been winning the most, but that's to be expected since he's been picking Manu's brain about the strengths of different players."

"He's winning?" Mauricio asked.

"Yeah. Like a lot. He even got a bonus a few weeks ago," Todd said. "You want in?"

"Nah. Not my thing," Mauricio said.

He chatted with his men for a few more minutes before he left. Why would Mal lie? And what was he hiding? Mauricio would have liked to let it go but he didn't want Helena to get hurt. And it wasn't just because he knew that Hadley would kill him if he let anything happen to her sister.

Seven

Hadley ran the wedding errands assigned by her mother and drove back to her shop just in time to meet the deliverymen who had brought the shipment of paintings from El Rod, an up-and-coming Western portrait artist whose work had recently been generating a lot of buzz. The paintings were raw and captured the wildness of the lives of the people who lived in southern New Mexico. He was from Taos and she'd only communicated with him via emails since he preferred not to use a phone.

She'd never considered herself a high-strung artist, but if she ever started selling her canvases for the amounts he was making, maybe she'd tell everyone not to call her. Too bad the one woman she didn't want to talk to—her mother—probably wouldn't be deterred by that type of edict.

She heard the bell on the door at the front of her shop jingle as she was opening the first crate. She put down the wedge she was using and looked over, surprised to see her sister standing there.

"What's up?"

"Um, shouldn't that be my question? I mean, I saw you dancing last night with Mauricio, but I thought you were smart enough to not let it go any further than that," Helena said.

"What makes you think that it did?" Hadley wasn't sure she was ready to talk to her sister about last night. Today she'd been trying so hard to focus on anything but that broken condom and the possible consequences.

All she'd been trying to do last night was get some closure with Mauricio. If she were a superstitious person, she'd probably assign some sort of greater meaning to what had happened.

"I was doing the books today at the Grand Hotel," Helena said. "The night manager saw me on his way out and told me how happy he was y'all had made up."

"Ugh. This is crazy. This morning half the people in the coffee shop thought the same thing," Hadley said.

Helena put her arm around Hadley and hugged her close. "Are you happy about whatever happened last night? Is this a good thing?"

"Oh, crapola," Hadley said. "It's complicated."

"That's what I thought. So, I brought lunch and figured we could talk," Helena said. "It's the least I could do after sticking you with Mom and the wedding."

Her sister squeezed her shoulder and showed her the insulated lunch bag from Famous Manu's BBQ. "Out here or in your office?"

Hadley started clearing one of the tables she used for her Wednesday night art classes and then drew over chairs for her and Helena.

"I really don't mind the wedding stuff. It's so much fun and different from the projects I normally work on," she said as she went to the little fridge under the counter and got out two sparkling waters.

Helena opened the bag of food and Hadley almost groaned. She had a weakness for the brisket from that place.

They sat across from each other eating in silence for a few minutes. When Hadley finally spoke, she dropped a bombshell.

"I might have gotten pregnant last night."

"Are you kidding me?"

"No. Mo's condom broke," Hadley said. "I'm going to get a pregnancy test but you know I can't buy one here or everyone will really lose their shit, especially Mom when it gets back to her."

"So, what are you going to do? You can't go to Dr. Phillips either," Helena said. She'd put her fork down and was staring at Hadley. "God, girl, when you do something, you don't do it by half measures, do you?"

"I don't. I mean, I never intend for stuff like this to happen, but it does. I really don't even know how."

"We'll figure this out," Helena said. "What does Mo think?"

"I don't know. We're having dinner tonight. He's apologized a ton but it's not like it's just his fault, you know?"

"I do know."

Hadley wiped her fingers on her napkin and put it down. "I'm going to Houston a week from Wednesday and I'll pick up a test there. I mean, until then it's not like knowing or not knowing is going to change anything."

Helena shook her head. "Not the outcome. But the truth is, just thinking you might be pregnant is probably doing something to your thoughts about Mo. And his about you. Leaving him was hard for you. Are you sure you don't want to consider other options?"

"Other options? No. That's not for me. It's not bothering me," Hadley said. "Why do you think it would?"

"Because having a man's baby is a big deal. Especially when that man is one that you can't seem to get over, even though you know there's no future with him," Helena said, sounding very much like a know-it-all older sister.

Hadley admitted Helena was saying the very thing she didn't want to acknowledge. "Whatever happens with that test, the truth is Mo and I have to figure out how to at least be friends again if we are going to both keep living here. I mean, if today is any example, then the town isn't ready for us to not be a couple either."

"I don't think the town cares who y'all are with as

long as you're happy. But you're always going to be in the spotlight, so get used to it. There isn't a person in this town who isn't connected to Mother and Mrs. Velasquez in some way or another."

She remembered her mom using her old cotillion date as leverage at the bakery and knew that Helena was right. She and Mo had to figure out how to co-exist and tonight would be a good first step toward figuring out how to be friends.

Just friends.

No matter how excited those crazy butterflies in her stomach were for her to see him again.

Mauricio helped Malcolm close the deal with the plastics people and they returned to the office. It was a little before five o'clock and quiet. A lot of his residential agents were out on appointments with clients who could only see the listings when they got off work.

He knew he should let Malcolm start the paperwork for the deal but he wanted some answers. It was one thing for Malcolm to not tell him about his money trouble, that he could understand, but lying about it? That wasn't like Malcolm at all. And put together with Helena's fears, it made Mauricio wonder what the hell was going on with his friend.

"So I had a chat with Todd today and he told me that our office is way ahead in the football league for the city," Mauricio said. "Now that's not what you told me, so I'm pretty damned sure one of you is lying to me. I don't give a crap about our football league standings, but if you felt the need to make something up, that does concern me."

Malcolm shook his head and leaned back against his desk, crossing his arms over his chest and his feet at the ankles. "Mo, it's not something I want to talk about. I'm sorry I lied to you about the league."

"Okay, fair enough. But if you hurt Helena because of this thing, I'm coming for you," he said.

"She's not yours to protect," Malcolm said, standing up.

"No, she's yours but you're clearly distracted," Mo said. "Get your shit together."

He turned and went into his office, closing the door behind him. He had no idea what kind of trouble Malcolm could be in, but for right now he was determined to do all he could to keep his friend safe and his engagement intact.

His phone pinged with a text message and he glanced down at it, hoping it wasn't Hadley canceling on him. Not that he'd blame her after the high-handed way he'd invited her to dinner.

But it was Diego reminding him he had polo practice tonight at six o'clock. He sent back the thumbs-up emoji and then texted his housekeeper, Rosalita, and asked her to bring a change of clothes and his toiletries bag to the polo grounds so he could shower and get dressed there.

Then he sat down at his desk just as the door to his office opened and his dad walked in. Domingo Velasquez took off his black Stetson as he entered

Mauricio's office and leaned one hip on the corner of his desk.

Mo had that sinking feeling in his gut that this wasn't a casual visit because his father was being too casual.

"Poppy, what are you doing here? Don't you have a standing round of drinks at the club at this time of day?" Mo asked. *Play it cool*, he warned himself.

"You know I do," he said. "But your mother saw you on Main Street at 4:49 this morning so we need to talk."

"Wow, that's precise," Mo said.

"I know. She wants to know what you were doing out at that hour and asked me to remind you that she would rather hear it from you than from the gossips when she goes to the club for dinner tonight," Domingo said. "So I'm here to get the scoop."

He took a deep breath and shook his head. "I went out with the boys last night to play pool at the Bull Pit and Hadley was there."

His father went stiff and turned to look more closely at Mauricio's hands. He seemed to relax when he didn't see any swelling or bruising on his knuckles. *Damn.* He wished he'd kept better control of his temper last year. "I wasn't fighting, Poppy. I ended up dancing with Hadley and one thing led to another. We had a lot to drink, so we walked to the Grand Hotel and then I went back for my car to take her home. That's when Mom saw me."

His dad stood up and walked over to the plate glass windows that looked down on the park. He turned his hat in his hands and didn't say anything. When Mauricio had been in trouble when he was younger, he'd always kept talking to fill the silence. But honestly, he had nothing more to say to his dad. He wasn't sure what would happen next with Hadley.

"Was it a one-time thing?" his father asked, his voice low and gravelly.

"I don't know. I don't want it to be, but I'm not sure what she wants. I'm taking her to dinner tonight," he said. "Also I'm not sure she will ever be able to forgive me. Or if I can prove to her that I'm worthy of her trust."

"Dinner is a good place to start. I know how this town is, but you have to do what's right for y'all. So if you need time or if that was what you needed to move on, I understand," his father said.

"Thank you," Mauricio said. "I just don't want her to get hurt again because of me."

"No man does," Domingo said.

"Does it ever get easier?" he asked his dad.

"Not really, and just wait until you have kids. If you have a daughter, it gets even worse," he said.

After his father left, his words echoed in Mauricio's mind. What if he did have a daughter with Hadley? He hadn't thought beyond a baby and what it would mean if she was pregnant. But a daughter—one who looked like Hadley—that would be a challenge. He knew how men would react to her and he wasn't sure his temper was ready for that. Or if it would ever be. Also what if he let down his daughter? He wanted to believe he'd changed, but he wasn't sure he was ready for fatherhood.

The Peace Creek Steak House was just off Main Street. Hadley realized if they wanted to keep a low profile, she shouldn't have suggested this place, but it wasn't as though most of the people who knew their families hadn't already cottoned on to the fact that something was going on. And she'd always been more of a face-it-head-on kind of girl.

Mauricio had shaved and changed into a gray suit that was clearly custom-made, paired with fancy leather boots. He held a Stetson in his left hand that perfectly matched his suit. His collar was open and she saw his St. Christopher medallion nestled in the hollow of his throat.

He put his hand on the small of her back as she followed their hostess to the table that was tucked into one of the alcoves near the back. She wished she'd chosen a wool dress instead of the light silk halter dress that left her back naked. But she'd wanted to look good for him and the touch of his hand on her skin did feel nice. Too nice.

They were in a nebulous no-man's-land and she wasn't sure what would happen next. But she'd promised herself no more free passes to hop into bed with Mo. She needed to be thinking with her head and not her vagina.

He held the chair out for her and then took a seat across the table as the waiter placed her napkin over her lap and then asked for their drink order. She started to order her customary glass of wine but then thought of why they were here. She could be expecting his baby. Better play it safe.

"Sparkling water with a twist of lime," Hadley said.

"Same," Mauricio said, and she heard the amusement in his voice. "On the wagon?" he asked once the waiter left.

"No. Just in case it turns out I'm…you know, I figure I'd better not take any chances," she said.

He sank back in his chair. "Good thinking. So, should we jump right into this discussion or what?"

"I think we should wait until we get our drinks, so we don't have any awkward waiter intrusions," she said.

He nodded again, and she realized that he was nervous, which was silly when she thought about all the dates they'd been on together. But the truth was, she'd always been hyper aware of everyone watching them, of trying to give the impression that they were the perfect couple. There had been so much pressure that, honestly, she couldn't remember a single meal where she hadn't been upset with Mo over something he hadn't done correctly.

"How was your day?" he asked after a minute of silence.

"Not too bad after you left me alone with Mother," she said, arching her eyebrows and sending him a look.

"Sorry about that. But Candace never really

warmed to me, and I had a feeling if I stayed, it wasn't going to be a good experience for anyone."

"You're probably right," Hadley said. Her mother really had liked Mauricio when they'd first started dating, but she'd gotten frustrated with how they had always broken up and then gotten back together. "She just thought we were like oil and water."

"She's wrong there. We were always like fire."

They *were* like fire, something that she'd never been able to control. The passion had always been the easy part between the two of them and so she'd felt that she had to work harder on the other stuff. It made her realize how immature she'd been, trying to make them perfect to the outside world instead of perfect for each other.

"So, after you dealt with your mother, what did you do?"

"I got a shipment from an artist I'm exhibiting next week. He's really hot right now. And I'm lucky to have gotten him. There's an invitation-only showing next Friday. I sent out the announcement to all the big-time collectors in the state. Would you like to come?"

"I would. What if we aren't…"

She put her hands on the table next to her plate and looked over at him, seeing the same uncertainty in his eyes that she felt deep inside. "No matter what, I think you and I have to figure out how to be friends. Unless one of us is leaving Cole's Hill. But I don't think that's going to happen."

"How do we do that, Had?" he asked just as the waiter brought their drinks.

Luckily, it gave her a reprieve from answering because she had no idea what to say. She wondered if too much had passed between them for them to ever just be friends but she hoped not. They could surely figure this out. Especially if she was pregnant. They were going to have to do something more than just be polite to each other. She wanted them to be friends, at least.

But how could she trust him? Really trust him? She wanted to believe he'd changed but was it permanent or was it simply that he felt bad for hurting her? Was it at his core?

"Hadley?"

"Hmm?"

"Have you decided what you want to eat?" Mauricio asked.

She hadn't even looked at the menu tonight but had been here so many times over the course of her life that she knew what she was going to have. She ordered the four-ounce filet mignon with the chef's special sauce, which had a creamy peppercorn flavor. After the waiter left, she realized that next Mo was going to want to talk about what they should do if the pregnancy test was positive.

She didn't want that. She wasn't sure that she could talk about a hypothetical and honor whatever agreement they made before she knew if the pregnancy was real or not. She only knew that she wasn't ready to walk away from Mauricio and that she was going to do her best to figure out if that meant starting a friendship with him or something more.

"So…"

"Would you mind terribly if we didn't discuss this tonight?" she asked. She was sort of surprised that she'd blurted out what was on her mind instead of doing as she usually did, which was accommodating him. Trying to guess what he wanted.

"Not at all. I thought you wanted to talk about it," he said.

"Not until we have to," she said. "Now tell me about your day."

"It wasn't too bad. I'm working on a few details for a new charity project and I had a showing on the Dunwoody mansion."

"I love that house. Is it as gorgeous inside as it used to be?"

"It's still nice but everything is dated. They could probably use someone like you to update the interior," he said.

"I don't do houses," she said.

"Not professionally but what you did at the house we shared was really good. Relaxing and elegant."

"Maybe too relaxing," she said without thinking.

"Probably. Made me think I didn't have to worry about you," he said. "But I should have, Hadley. I'll be honest. I think I took advantage of you because you were always so accommodating."

"I think I let you," she admitted. "I wanted what my parents have and for some reason I thought if I made life easy for you, you'd do the same."

"I wish I had," he admitted.

She just nodded. "The food here is really good."

He let her change the topic and they talked about the high school football team and the new menu at Famous Manu's but she couldn't help noticing that Mo got quieter and a little tenser.

As the evening wore on, she realized that by relaxing and being herself, she was enjoying her time with Mauricio more than she had in the entire last year they'd dated. She was able to concentrate on what he was saying and realized he was a really good storyteller. As the evening ended, she felt that no matter what the outcome of the pregnancy test, the two of them were setting up the bonds of a true friendship.

Eight

After dinner, Mauricio suggested they tour the new polo grounds and stables that he and Diego had recently opened on the outskirts of Cole's Hill. He was happy when she said yes.

"Diego and Bartolome Figueras are both the experts when it comes to horses and polo but I still wanted to invest and be a full partner in the facility," he said as they drove through the quiet town. Bart was a famed polo player and model from Argentina. He'd been friends with the Velasquez family for years.

"I'm glad you are. You always wanted to be more than the man who makes the real estate deals," she said.

His ego perked up that she remembered that tidbit about him. But he knew that was simply because she tended to listen when he talked. He wished he could say the same about himself. He didn't know as many details about her from their time together.

"What about you?" he asked. "I know you have the exhibit, and Bianca mentioned you do some sort of class once a week."

Hadley rested her head against the leather seat and turned to stare out the window at the passing landscape.

"Yes, I have the Wednesday night drawing class for serious artists and I'm thinking of adding a Mommy-Daddy-and-Me art class either after school or on the weekends," she said. "I'm still trying to figure out what I want the shop to be. I don't need to make a profit at this moment in time because I'm still working with one of my bigger clients in Manhattan so that covers the bills, and I own the property where the shop and loft are outright—thanks to you. I never would have thought to invest in real estate if you hadn't made me."

He couldn't help the chuckle that escaped him. "Darling, no man on this planet has ever made you do anything. The word *stubborn* was invented for you."

He glanced over to see her smiling to herself. "You are just used to women taking one look at your muscles and charming smile and giving in to whatever you suggest. I'm...discerning."

He had been used to that. From the very beginning, Hadley had been different and he liked the challenge of her. She kept him on his toes.

"You are certainly that," he agreed, turning off the main FM road toward the polo grounds.

He pulled up to the main building containing the stables and put the car in Park. "I need to text Diego and let him know I'm here so he doesn't come out if the alarm goes off."

"Sure," she said. "I'm going to walk over there by the fence. I've been wanting to see the new grounds."

He nodded. As she got out of the car, he followed her, texting his brother, who simply told him to have fun and make sure he locked up when he left. Then he caught up to Hadley where she leaned against the fence. The breeze caught her hair, pulling at it and drawing it away from her face. She had her head tipped back and his breath caught in his chest. She was too good for him, but he still wanted her more than anything in this world. She'd always made him a better man and he'd never realized that until he'd lost her.

He raised his phone, snapped a picture of her and then pocketed it. He knew himself well enough to guess he'd screw this up again and he wanted a record of this moment when they were getting along perfectly and nothing else had intruded.

She glanced over her shoulder at him as he approached. "Did you get permission, or do we have to keep an eye out for Johnny Law?"

"When have you ever had to worry about the cops?" he asked. If there was a poster child for being a good girl, Hadley was it. She was a rule follower and stickler for doing things properly.

"Never," she admitted. "It doesn't even make me embarrassed. I hate that feeling I get when I know I'm doing something I shouldn't."

"Like what?"

"Dancing with you," she said.

"Touché."

"I'm just saying you feel dangerous to me. You make me… Well, that's not fair. It's not you making me do anything. Around you, I just forget my normal self and the things I do to make my life comfortable… I'm just making it worse, aren't I?"

"No, you're not. I think I like that something about me makes you uncomfortable, unless you meant it in a negative way. Did you?"

She turned around, leaning back against the fence with her arms on the top railing. "No, I didn't. Most of the time I like being the good girl, the one who knows all the rules of etiquette and how to act in public. But with you, I also feel edgy. Like I should throw all of that out and just be…different. Just take a chance."

He wanted her to take a chance—on him. He'd been thinking about her a lot since they'd broken up. He knew they'd been young when they'd first hooked up. They both came from good families so everyone thought they were a good match but, honestly, he'd never really taken the time to find out what it was they had in common beyond upbringing.

And it was an opportunity he wasn't going to waste again.

* * *

Hadley hadn't meant to be as honest as all that with Mo. Not tonight and maybe not ever. There was something that made her feel vulnerable when she stepped out of the shadow of her very proper mother and let her real self shine through. She wasn't ever going to be fully comfortable with that. But with Mo, who had seen her at her best and arguably at her absolute worst, she sort of had no choice.

"What about you?" she asked. "Do I do anything to you?"

"Other than turn me on?" he asked.

She glanced away. Of course, he'd bring it back to the physical. She bared her soul and he wanted to talk about the ridiculously hot passion that had always been between them.

"Hey," he said, coming over and putting his hand on her upper arm. "I'm sorry. I guess what you do is make me feel vulnerable. Like I have something that I don't want to let go of, and instead of reacting like a grown-up, I fall back to being a teenage boy with the hots for the prettiest girl in Cole's Hill."

She felt her heart soften a little toward him. She didn't know if he was playing her right now but she was going to take him at his word. "I'm not the prettiest, I can tell you that. I mean, Helena is gorgeous, your sister was a supermodel—"

"You are to me. I don't know about either of them. Since they're sisters to us, I don't see them the way I see you. And truthfully, it's not just those two, Had. I don't see other women the way I see you. Something about you is just…perfect for me."

"Then why was Marnie in your room?"

"I missed you," he said. "I wasn't sure you were ever coming back. You know I had texted you and you never responded."

"I didn't," she admitted. "I was afraid we'd just continue the rest of our lives breaking up and getting back together…but then I was in Cole's Hill and I had to see you. I know that part of this was my fault—"

"No. It was me," he said. "I cared about you back then and I still do today. I shouldn't have slept with anyone else."

The evening breeze stirred around them and she tipped her head back, taking in the moon and the seriousness in his eyes.

"Do you mean that?"

"I do," he said, drawing his hand down her arm and leaving gooseflesh in its wake. He linked their fingers together and started walking across the paddock toward the main building. "Remember when we first started dating and I used to always look at you?"

"Yes. I think I said stop staring at me, creeper," she said with a laugh.

"You did," he confirmed. "But a part of me couldn't believe you were mine, that you'd picked me out of all the other men you could have chosen. I kept looking at you to see if you had regrets, and I'm pretty sure that's where our troubles started. I never felt like I was enough for you."

She stopped walking and looked over at him.

"Mauricio Velasquez, million-dollar deal maker, son of one of the most prestigious Five Families…you were enough. Sometimes more than enough. You can be very intense."

He dropped her hand. "We should have talked about this, shouldn't we have?"

"Probably, but we weren't ready for that. I had this image in my head of what kind of couple we should be, you had something you wanted us to be too, and we are both very competitive when it comes to our careers. I think talking would have been hard when we were together."

He turned away and started walking again and she fell into step beside him until they got to the barn where the horses were kept. He entered a code and then held the door open for her as she walked inside. She realized that something she'd said bothered him, and as he moved silently past her to turn on the light, she wished she knew what it was. They were never going to be one of those totally in sync couples like Helena and Malcolm were or like his sister, Bianca, and her husband. Was it her?

"Listen, I'm sorry if I said something that upset you," she began.

"Stop. I'm a man, not some wuss. I don't get upset," he said.

"What do you get then?" she asked, because he was clearly out of sorts. When her daddy got like this, her mother would send him out to his man cave until he could be *decent*, to put it in her mom's famous words.

"Pissed off. And I'm not pissed at you, darling, but at myself for thinking I'm even worthy of you, that we could be rebuilding a relationship."

She realized they needed to talk. She wasn't sure what she wanted from this. Friendship, of course. That was a must, no matter how much further it went.

She went over to a stall where one of the horses had come and put its nose over the railing. She held her hand out for the horse to smell her first, and then once it seemed to accept her, she pet it.

If there were only some way of doing that with Mo. Some signal he could give her of what he wanted.

"I'm not sure what's going on between us," she began, her own voice low in part not to startle the horse but also because she wasn't sure of what she was saying. "Today I realized that we're going to have to be friends. Then tonight as we talked at dinner and I had a really good time, I hope it's the start of a new phase for us."

She looked over at him where he stood in the middle of the aisle with his hands on his hips just watching her. She wanted to trust him. The lights made his black hair look darker than midnight. It was so thick, she wished she could reach out and thread her fingers through it like she was doing to the horse's mane.

"If I'm pregnant, that will force us into making choices we might not have made. But if I'm not, I still want to work on our friendship."

He wanted that too. But he felt like he was already letting her down. He didn't do conversations about emotions well, and the only emotions he'd ever really felt at ease with were anger or passion. But he knew that wasn't going to be enough. Not with Hadley. Not this time.

There was a reason why they kept breaking up each time they tried again. And she was so right when she said that the baby—if there was one—would complicate things.

"I want that too. I'm not going to pretend I don't want to sleep with you and that I'm not thinking about last night every time I look at you. I mean, I'm smart enough to know that's not what either of us needs right now, but that doesn't mean I don't want you."

She smiled at him. It was the sweetest smile he'd seen on her face in a long time, like the one she'd worn last night when she'd been sleeping in his arms and he thought he'd done something right. Like he'd said the right thing. But what the hell was it?

"I want you too. But I think that's gotten in our way over the years. It's so easy to fall into each other's arms instead of talking things through. For both of us," she said. "But if you're on the same page as I am, why don't we try the friends thing, no matter what the outcome of the test—which I will go to Houston and pick up."

Friends.

"Is this you friend-zoning me? Or are you saying if we're friends first, we'll be a stronger couple if we get to that stage later?" he asked.

"The second one. I want you too, Mo. That's never been an issue. I really want to figure out how to live together in this small town of ours, and if we have a kid to raise together, we have to know how to do that. That's got to be the first thing."

What she said made sense. Even though he had been hoping to get her into his arms again tonight, he could wait if it meant that this time if they got back together, it would last.

He was getting to the age where a crazy roller-coaster relationship wasn't what he wanted. Maybe it was seeing his brother getting married or spending so much time with his nephew, but he knew he wanted something more substantial for this next phase of his life. His thirties…that's when his dad had always said it was time to grow up.

"Okay," he said. "Let's do this friend thing."

"Okay…so what do we do now?" she asked.

"Don't ask me. I'm still trying to stop thinking about kissing you again. And how much I want to pull you into my arms."

"Stop that," she said, wagging her finger at him. "Now you've got me thinking about it too."

"Good," he said with a wink. "Want to go for a ride? Or should I take you home?"

"Home, I think," she said after a pause. "But I do want to come back and tour the polo grounds. When is your next match?"

"Two weeks," he said. "We're doing a charity match against Bartolome and his team. It will be for fun, but you know we don't want to lose."

"When have you and your brothers ever approached a sport as just *fun*?"

"Never. We picked a date when Inigo wasn't going

to be racing and could come home to play with us. He's technically not allowed to do anything high risk, which is why we're just saying this is an informal match." She shook her head and he just shrugged. "We're all rule breakers."

"I know that, Mo, believe me. For some reason it's one of the things I like about you."

"I'd never do anything to put anyone in danger," he said, as he led her out of the stables and turned out the lights. They walked over to his car in silence and when he opened her door for her, she brushed past him and then she stopped.

Her breath caught between her parted lips as a shiver of sensual need went through him. He leaned down before he could stop himself and brushed his lips over hers. Then he felt her hands on either side of his face as she kissed him back before she broke the contact between them and got into the car.

He closed the door and turned to walk around behind it, stopping for a minute to take several deep breaths to center himself. How was he ever going to manage being just friends? He couldn't think of a time when he was next to her that he didn't want to reach out and touch her, kiss her, pull her into his arms and never let her go.

But he had to.

If he wanted her to stay in Cole's Hill for good this time, he had to figure it out.

Did he want her to stay for good?

He was pretty damned sure he did.

He got into the car. When he started the engine,

she reached over and fiddled with the radio until she found a country western station. The music filled the car on the drive home and he did a pretty good job of forgetting he wanted her until Eric Church's "Like a Wrecking Ball" came on.

He almost thought that Hadley wasn't affected until she reached over and pushed the button to change the channel to a Top Forty station. But the damage had been done. He remembered her pressed against him last night at the Bull Pit, dancing so close that he felt every inch of her.

When he finally pulled into her parking space at her loft, she looked over at him.

"Thanks for a nice night," she said, dashing out of the car before he could say anything more.

Nine

Hadley woke to her phone pinging and someone knocking on her door. She groaned and rolled over to look at the clock. It was eight in the morning. Not exactly early but she hadn't slept well last night, dreaming of Mauricio and regretting not taking that kiss further than she had.

The knocking continued, and she grabbed her phone as she hopped out of bed. Her Ravenclaw boxers and *Also, I Can Kill You With My Brain* T-shirt were respectable enough for whoever was trying to wake her up.

She glanced at her phone and saw that her sister was texting and as she glanced in the peephole, she remembered it was Tuesday.

Tuesday morning.

She was supposed to meet her mother at Kinley's to help her and Helena finalize the floral bouquet choices. Hadley had done a few design sketches and sent them over to Kinley, who was having samples made for them to look at.

She opened the door and stepped back as her mother brushed past her into the apartment. It had an open floor plan, and though her bed had two decorative screens that blocked it from the view of the living room, her mother went straight to it and then came back out as Hadley moved into the kitchen area, starting a pot of coffee. She had a feeling she was going to need at least ten cups to face her mother this morning.

"I'm not interested in excuses. I thought you were dead," Candace said, setting her Birkin bag on the table near the front door before coming over and standing next to the kitchen island.

"I had a long night working on my project for the company in New York. I slept through my alarm, Mom. No excuse, but I'm sorry," Hadley said, going over and giving her mom a hug that she immediately returned, squeezing Hadley close.

"I really thought something had happened to you. You are never late and then I couldn't get you on the phone," Candace said. She kissed Hadley's temple and then stepped back, blinking as she reached up to touch her chignon.

Hadley hadn't realized at first how much it had freaked her mom out when she hadn't shown up. But then she was the reliable sister. The one who never said no and was always there. "Again, I'm very sorry. Why did you check the bedroom?"

"Mavis Crandall saw you out with Mo last night and I was just checking to see if he was why you were late," she said.

"No. We're trying to get past the breakup and be friends," Hadley said, checking the glass coffeepot and seeing there was already enough for a mug of coffee. She grabbed two earthenware mugs that she'd gotten from a local artist on Main Street and put one under the drip while pouring out the coffee into the other one.

"Want a cup?" she asked her mom.

"I can't. I already had one today," she said. "I'd love some juice if you have it."

"I do. Have a seat and let me get it for you," Hadley said. "Did you reschedule for today?"

"I tried to but Kinley isn't available until Thursday," her mother said in a tone that told Hadley she was put out by the fact that Kinley wouldn't reschedule her other clients.

Hadley wasn't surprised by that. Kinley wasn't one to back down and was used to dealing with bridezillas who made her mom look like a saint.

"How about I make it up to you by taking you to brunch?"

"Sounds good. I'll text Helena and ask her to join us," Candace said.

"She might be working, Mom," Hadley pointed out.

"Nonsense. She's her own boss. She can take a

break and have brunch with us. I'll call the club while you shower and make sure they have the table I like by the window. Oh, this is going to be so nice," she said.

Hadley got her mom her juice, then took her coffee into her bedroom area to get ready. She heard her mom on the phone being as sweet as could be but not hesitating to coerce first Helena into joining them and then the maître d' at the club into reserving her favorite table.

Hadley took a quick shower, got dressed and applied a light bit of makeup to cover the evidence of her sleepless night. Then she rejoined her mother, who looked perfectly at ease moving around the apartment fluffing pillows.

"I think it's time you redid your place," Candace said. "It looks like you just threw everything in here. I know that when you moved out of Mauricio's you didn't really have the time to pick out nice pieces, but now that it looks like you're staying, we should get you some good furniture."

Her mom had a point. No matter what happened with her and Mauricio, she was going to need to make this place her home. And her mom was right: she'd simply looked at the loft as temporary. It had been a stopgap after she'd moved back from New York, unsure of what she was going to do next.

"I might need to take a trip to the antique markets," Hadley said.

"I'll reach out to my contacts and see what's available," Candace said. "There's nothing I love more than shopping for my girls."

Hadley smiled as they both grabbed their handbags and left the apartment. She'd been so busy thinking about the baby in terms of how it would impact her and Mo that she hadn't considered what it might be like to be a mom…like her mother.

She followed her mom's Audi as she drove through town to the Five Families Country Club, but her mind wasn't on the drive, it was on the child. What if she was really pregnant? She'd have a baby of her own. Someone she could dote on the way her parents always had.

For the first time since she'd looked at that broken condom, she had the thought that maybe being pregnant wasn't the worst thing to happen. Sure, she and Mauricio could be closer, but they were working on that. And a child…of her own? Someone who was hers? That was one thing she'd never realized she'd been missing.

Brunch with her mom and her sister was the last thing that Helena wanted to do today. For one thing, Malcolm's behavior was getting more and more erratic and she would have a difficult time fooling either of them that she wasn't stressed out. She could put it down to wedding jitters. Yeah, she thought, that was the excuse she'd use if one of them brought it up.

She used some undereye concealer and highlighter on her cheeks to try to make herself look peppier, but to be honest, when she looked at her reflection in the rearview mirror, she knew she hadn't really hidden her inner turmoil.

Her mom and sister were already inside the country club. Even if Hadley hadn't been texting Where are you? every thirty seconds for the last ten minutes, she knew they were inside thanks to their cars parked side by side in the lot. She had asked her assistant to text her after thirty minutes and say there was an emergency so she wouldn't have to stay the entire time.

"So you weren't dead," Hadley said to Helena as she joined her mom and sister at their usual corner table near the large windows that overlooked the golf course.

"I wasn't," Helena said.

"I told you," Hadley said, giving her mom a pointed look.

"You girls have no idea what it's like to be a mom. When I text or call you and get no response, my first reaction is to run through a long list of everything that could be wrong, starting with kidnapping and ending with death."

Helena reached over and squeezed her mom's hand. "We know you worry but you need to remember we're your daughters. Anyone who comes for us better be ready for a fight."

"I know. Doesn't stop me from worrying," her mom said. "Hadley was just telling me she has to run to Houston for a client next week and I asked her to go back to the flower district and speak to Manuel to find out what blooms will be the freshest in December for your wedding."

"Thanks, sis," Helena said. She should probably try to get Hadley alone and see if she was doing okay with the whole might-be-pregnant thing.

"No problem. I'm pretty sure that Kinley will have some good ideas too," Hadley said.

"If she'd had time to talk to us today, then we'd know that," Candace said.

Helena fought to hide her smile. Her mother didn't like it when the world didn't bend to her demands. Their daddy had said more than once it was his fault for treating her like a princess when they'd been dating, but Helena didn't buy that at all. Her mother had always had a steel backbone and demanded excellence.

"She has other clients, Mom. It will be fine," Helena said.

"Of course it will. And it was our fault that we missed the first one," Candace agreed. "Now, what's going on with my girls? I'm so glad we're getting this time to catch up."

"Well, I had to rearrange my work schedule this morning," Helena said. "Apparently my sister was in mortal danger but everything is great now."

"You have your daddy's smartass humor, Helena. It's not as attractive as either of y'all believe it is," Candace said, rolling her eyes and then taking a sip of her sparkling water.

"That's one opinion. Had, what do you think?"

"I'm going to have to side with Mom on this one. It's funny to hear you joke about someone else but when you direct it at me, I'm not a huge fan," Hadley said.

"I'll try to remember that. So what were you doing last night?" Helena asked as the waiter placed an avocado salad in front of her. "Were you out with Mo again?"

"I was, as you know. We're trying to be friends," Hadley said, looking down at her plate and pushing the lettuce around. Helena felt a little mean for bringing him up.

"How's that going?" Candace asked.

"Well, we're taking it slowly. I invited him to the art exhibit I'm having next week at the shop, and he invited me to a polo match that he's participating in. He apologized for the other-woman thing. He's trying to show me he's changed."

"Relationships take work, but make sure you are both doing it."

"We are. I'm not going to just fall for him saying things are different."

"Glad to hear that," Helena said.

"Sounds like y'all are making a good second start," Candace said.

But to Helena it sounded like her sister was playing a careful game. Helena knew how hard it was to manage a man when there were variables out of her control. In her case, it was whatever the hell Malcolm was up to; in Hadley's, maybe a baby.

"Thanks, Mom. I think so too," Hadley said. "Helena, are you and Malcolm going to Bianca's baby shower on Saturday?"

"We plan to," she said, but who knew if her fiancé was going to be reliable? She needed to sit him down and force him to tell her what was going on, but the truth was, she was starting to think he'd changed his mind about marrying her and a part of her didn't want to know.

Of course, she didn't want to get left at the altar either. She was nervous about what it was that was taking up so much of his time and money and would eventually have to confront him about it.

"Good. I was going to send a present and my regrets, but since you're going, I think I'll attend."

The conversation drifted to Kinley Caruthers who rumor had it might have let her husband, Nate, out of the doghouse after he bought their four-year-old Penny a four-wheeler and let her sit on his lap and drive it around the yard.

Helena laughed but her heart was heavy. All she wanted was to be like Bianca or Kinley, starting a life with the man she loved, not sitting over here like Nancy Drew trying to solve the mystery of what was going on with him.

When Mauricio got home from work that evening, Alec was waiting in his apartment. His twin brother looked harried and not his usual self. Mauricio undid his tie as he walked through the living room where Alec was sprawled on the couch watching ESPN.

"Hope you don't mind if I crash here," Alec said. "I would have called first, but I came from the airport."

"I don't mind," Mo said. "What's up?"

"Today is the release of the latest update," Alec said. "This time I might have bitten off more than I could chew."

Alec was a software genius who wrote code that handled everything you could imagine. His house in the Five Families subdivision was completely auto-mated. But each time his company had a new release, Alec, who was normally the most confident of guys, was nervous.

"Is it a tequila or beer night?"

"Tequila," Alec said. "But I promised to take Benito so that Bianca and Derek could go to their prenatal class, so neither."

His brother kept flipping between all the sports channels, finally stopping on one that showed the Formula One rankings. Alec turned up the volume as they both turned their attention to the stats. Inigo was in the top five. Not surprising since he was a determined competitor who'd been driving since he was a teenager.

When the rankings story was over, Alec turned the volume down. He knew that Alec needed to be distracted. Otherwise, he'd just sit here worrying about the reaction to his latest release, which would be happening on the West Coast this evening at four o'clock…so any minute now.

"I'll drive. Let's get Beni and go play some polo. Text Diego and tell him to meet us there," Mauri-cio said.

"I'm not sure I'm up for—"

"You're not. So, I'm going to suggest you play on

Diego's team," Mo said with a wink. He and Alec had never been those twins who felt each other's exact emotions, but they were empathetic with each other. Both of them knew when the other one was dealing with something bigger than normal.

"Ha. Okay. You're right. Sitting here stewing isn't going to help," Alec said. "Which makes me wonder how you knew that. You're not normally the intuitive twin."

He shrugged at his brother. What could he say? He could relate to needing a distraction. He'd been keeping as busy as he could until Hadley let him know if she was pregnant or not. Then it occurred to him that he hadn't told anyone about it. But what would he say to them if she wasn't?

"What is it?" Alec said. "I've been having weird dreams again."

Damn.

The one thing that had always linked them was their dreams. Neither of them had ever been comfortable talking about it to their other brothers.

"Hadley might be pregnant," he said. "We won't know until she has a chance to go get a test."

"Wow. Okay, I wasn't expecting that. Do I need to give you the protection talk? I thought Dad covered it pretty well when he said no one likes using a condom but always use one."

Mauricio shoved his hands in his pockets and shook his head. "I did. It broke."

"Well, hell," Alec said.

"Exactly. And we aren't really in a place that I can

say we're a couple, which I know isn't good. Why do things like this always happen with Hadley?"

Alec studied him for a long moment. "We never talked about your breakup. I mean, I know the details of what happened…her walking in on you with Marnie. But what I mean is how it affected you. I never understood why you both broke up the first time."

Mauricio ran a hand through his hair. "I'll tell you while we go pick Benito up. If we're late, Bianca won't be very happy with us."

"True," Alec said. "I'll drive. I have the prototype of an electronic sports car that I designed the engine for."

"That's yours? I saw it in the garage. Me likey."

"Me too. They are going to go into production in the fall. Want me to put you down for one?"

"Hell, yeah," Mo said. They took the private elevator to the garage and Alec got behind the wheel. For a few moments, they listened to the radio and Mauricio thought his brother had forgotten about their conversation.

"So what happened with her?" Alec asked when they were headed toward the Five Families subdivision.

Mauricio took a deep breath. "I want to say I don't know, but the truth is, I think I started to take her for granted. You know Hadley. She looks nice all the time, she scheduled all of our social events, she has a good career and she made our place really comfortable. And I thought that she'd keep doing all of that and I'd just be me."

Just be me. Like he was such a prize that she'd keep on giving her all to a man who wasn't really checked in to the relationship.

"She just got tired of asking me to be a part of the couple and said we needed a break. Instead of seeing it as a wake-up call, I thought it was my chance to be a single guy until she came to her senses and returned to me."

"Damn. I know I'm the smart one, but I never thought of you as dumb until you said that," Alec said.

"I know. I hate that part of myself," Mo admitted. "But you know me. I always think I'm God's gift."

"You're being too hard on yourself. I'm sure there is more to it than what you've said. But now that you know what's wrong, you can fix it," Alec said. "Don't discount yourself, Mo. I know you, and you've always adapted when you need to. If you want Hadley back for good, you'll figure it out."

He hoped so. Because as he'd been vocalizing what had gone wrong, he realized that he wasn't the same man he'd been eighteen months ago when she'd left. He'd changed. And partying and his image as a player used to seem so important weren't compared to having Hadley in his life.

Ten

Hadley got back from Houston later than she expected thanks to the traffic, which was no one's fault but her own thanks to her dawdling at one of the large shopping centers on the outskirts. At least she had the test; there was no more putting it off. She could take it and find out the results. But Mauricio wanted to be there when she did. She picked up her phone and sent him a text.

Back from H. Do you still want to come over when I take it?

He responded right away.

Yes. I can't be there until after nine.

Okay. Text me when you are on the way.

She put the test on the counter in the bathroom and walked away from it. It was six o'clock. That meant she had three hours to kill. Helena was working late since their mom had hijacked her workday earlier.

She texted Zuri and Josie to see if either of them wanted to meet for dinner or go to the gym.

She heard back from Josie first.

Dinner. I need to talk.

Then Zuri replied.

Gym? Who are you kidding? We aren't the gym type.

Hadley laughed as she typed.

Wanted to give you options. So where for dinner? I think I can get a table at Hinckleman's on short notice.

Her friends thought the farm-to-table restaurant was the perfect choice, so she texted the head chef who was a friend of hers and got them a table. Then she touched up her makeup and headed out. Hinckleman's was near the highway, which made it more convenient for the ranchers and farmers who didn't always like coming into town for dinner.

Josie was already seated in a highbacked booth when Hadley arrived.

"What's up?" she asked after they exchanged pleasantries.

"Z said if we talked without her, she'd shoot me. And you know, I think I believe her," Josie said.

"That's right. I did," Zuri said as she slid into the booth next to Hadley, hugging her and reaching across the table to squeeze Josie's hand. "Now spill. Is it about Manu? It has to be."

Hadley thought it was about the football coach, as well. Of all of them, Josie was the most cautious when it came to men and dating. Her mother had remarked one time that it was no doubt due to all the books that Josie read. They gave her higher standards when it came to the men she wanted to date.

"Yes, it is. He asked me to go with him to the Hall of Fame dinner this year. His team is getting an award," Josie said.

"I think there is only one answer and that's hell, yes," Zuri said with a toss of her head. As her long silky black hair swirled around her, the fragrance of roses wafted toward Hadley.

"No, there isn't. We've all seen what famous football players' wives and girlfriends look like and I don't fit the mold," Josie said.

The waitress arrived and they all ordered a glass of wine and their entrées. When she left, Josie didn't say anything.

"Okay, so do you want to go?" Hadley asked, realizing how grateful she was to have her good friends here tonight. When she'd moved to Manhattan, she lost touch with them, and when she came back, and everything had happened with Mauricio, she hadn't wanted to reach out with a problem. But they had both come to her when they'd realized she was back in town. It made her realize how lucky she was to have these women as friends.

"I think I do," she said. "It's an important night for him and I want to help him celebrate, but I don't want him to see me with other women and…"

"And what?" Zuri asked. "Because, girl, I know you're not trying to say that he might reconsider. That's an insult to you and to him."

"Don't you think I know that? I feel stupid even thinking that I might not be able to fit in with that group. I mean, I know that Ferrin is going to be there and she's super sweet and nice."

Ferrin Caruthers was the wife of former NFL bad boy Hunter Caruthers—Mo's brother-in-law. Hunter and Manu used to be teammates.

"Then it's not about who's going to be there, is it?" Hadley asked. "It's you. You're afraid that if you go, you're not going to be able to keep things casual with him."

Josie nibbled on her bottom lip. "I think you're right. I mean, we've both been very careful at school and it's not like dating is prohibited between teachers. But what if it doesn't work out?"

"What if it does?" Zuri asked. "You're one of the most solid people I know. You really know what you want and how to go after it."

"I do?" Josie said.

Hadley knew exactly how her friend felt. Once

emotions were involved, it was harder to trust that she was making a smart decision. "Definitely. We've known each other since Brownies. Z and I know you better than you know yourself at times. I think you're hesitating because once you commit to this, you'll be risking your heart."

Wow. It was so much easier to see it from the outside. But this was why she'd been reluctant to take the pregnancy test. She hadn't realized it until this moment. Taking the test meant things between Mauricio and her would change—one way or the other—and she wasn't completely sure she was ready for that.

"I agree," Zuri said. "When did Hadley get so smart?"

"When she got her heart broken," Josie said. "That's wisdom tempered by experience."

"Yes, it is. No reason y'all can't benefit from my mistakes," she said, but she wasn't sure she'd classify her time with Mo as a mistake.

"No reason at all. But I don't think it was all bad for you," Zuri said. "I mean, I'm pretty sure you guys are moving forward now, right?"

"Maybe," Hadley said. She wanted to see what happened tonight before she committed in front of her friends. "Josie, are you going to go to the awards dinner?"

The waitress dropped off their wine and some pimento cheese and crackers before Josie answered.

"Yes, I think I am."

After Alec had dropped him back off at his penthouse, Mauricio almost texted Hadley using the late-ness of the hour as an excuse not to stop by. But of course, that wasn't an option.

He'd changed.

Alec's launch had gone very well, which hadn't surprised any of them, and they'd ended up at their parents' house celebrating the good news. Mo felt better than he had in a long time. The breakup with Hadley had unmoored him, shaken the very foundations of his life. He'd been drifting for a while, even though he was keeping his business on top of the real estate market, working with his charities. And then last fall, he'd given into the jealousy and anger that came from seeing Hadley moving on, while he was stuck.

But tonight, he saw the seeds of his future, the man he was regardless of whether or not Hadley was pregnant. And that made him feel content. Which was something that had eluded him for way too long.

He was parked behind the retail shops where the entrance to Hadley's loft was located. He was sitting there in his Bugatti, letting the engine run, trying to decide if he should text first or just go up, when his phone pinged.

When are you going to be here?

I'm here. Was just fixing to text you.

Come on up, I'll buzz the door.

He got out of the car and walked to the security door Alec had designed. It had a camera and intercom for visitors, but for residents it had a retinal scan in case they forgot their key.

The door buzzed and unlocked as soon as he was in sight of the camera, which meant she'd been watching for him.

He took the elevator up to the residential area. There were only six loft apartments in the building. He was still hoping to develop another plot of land opposite this one with a similar structure. Hadley owned the adjoining land, so maybe that was a project they could work on together.

He knocked on her door when he got to it and she opened it, stepping back for him to enter. He realized she was in an odd mood. And he totally got it. He wasn't too sure what he wanted the outcome of the test to be.

"How was your day?" he asked, trying to be chill.

"Okay. I slept through my alarm. My mom thought that I was dead and came over here banging on the door to wake me up," Hadley said. "But otherwise not bad."

He had to laugh at that. "Moms always think the worst."

"They really do. I pointed out that I'm pretty tough, but she said she can't help panicking."

"I get it. I think I'd probably react the same if I couldn't get in touch with you. You're usually so reliable."

"That's me," she said. "Reliable."

There was a sadness… Maybe that wasn't the right

word, but there was something in the way she said it that made him realize she was in a funk.

"Hey, there's nothing wrong with being reliable. I like that about you. In fact, it's probably one of the things that I took for granted when we were together. Like because you were solid I didn't need to be. I'm sorry about that."

She went into her living room area and took a seat in the large armchair, crossing her legs underneath her. He sat down on the matching couch. Her apartment was a hodgepodge of furniture that seemed to come from one of those furniture places that sold pieces by the room. It was nice, but it wasn't Hadley with her artsy eclectic taste.

"Thank you for apologizing for that," she said after a minute. "I think I sort of wanted us to be this picture-perfect couple too, so I was forcing both of us into things that weren't really us."

He didn't know about that, but just nodded. "So…"

"I guess I should just go do it," she said.

"If you want to," he said. "Do you want to talk first?"

"I don't know," she said at last. "I mean, chances are really slim that I'll be pregnant, you know?"

"I do. But that hasn't stopped me from thinking about a baby with you, darling," he admitted.

"And what do you think?"

"I keep coming back to the fact that I have rotten timing when it comes to you," he said. "I don't want anything to complicate this new thing you and I have going."

She nodded. "Me neither."

"So whatever happens, I don't want to go back to living separate lives," he said.

"Okay. Whatever happens, we won't," she agreed. "Let me go pee on the stick now. I'll let you know when it's done."

When she stood up, he did, as well. Reaching out to catch her hand, he drew her into his arms, wrapping them around her until they were pressed together. He rubbed his hands down her back and then leaned down to kiss her long and slow, because this was a moment that they'd never have again. One where they were on the cusp. He wanted to remember it forever.

She returned his kiss, her hands tunneling through his hair and holding his head so that she could deepen the embrace as she came up on tiptoe. Then slowly she pulled back and stepped away.

He watched her walk toward the large screens that concealed her bedroom and her bathroom. He followed her after a minute, sitting down on her bed, feeling more awkward than he had before. At least the last time they'd thought she might be pregnant, they'd been living together and thought they had a future together.

This time was so different. They already knew they could screw up a relationship and that made it harder to believe they could make it work this time.

She stared at the negative result for too long. The ache in her gut was a mix of relief and regret. Bittersweet, like so many things with Mauricio. Well, at least it would be much easier on both of them to not have to figure out a baby in the midst of everything.

When she opened the bathroom door, he took one look at her face and stood up, coming over to her.

"No?"

"Yeah," she said, feeling an odd burn of tears at the back of her eyes. She blinked a few times to keep them from falling. It wasn't as if she wanted to be pregnant. Really. Or was it?

"Well, hell," Mo said. "I'm not as relieved as I thought I'd be."

She nodded. She wasn't sure what she felt. He pulled her into his arms, hugging her close. She hugged him back and realized that there was something solid about Mauricio. She felt like she could count on him and that was new. There was so much familiar between them but this new thing, well, it made her realize how much he'd changed.

"Obviously, this was for the best," he said, but it felt like…well, like they'd missed a shot at having an excuse to get back together. Not just to be friends like she'd suggested, but as a real couple.

He stood back, realizing that when it came to Hadley, he always hesitated. And maybe that was why they'd always been on again, off again.

"I'm going to lay it on the line, Hadley," he started, and she looked up at him with one of those expressions that always kept him guessing about what she was really thinking.

"Okay."

"I'm disappointed, but more because if you'd been pregnant, I'd have had a reason to call you and be with you and I don't think we would need an excuse to be together. I want to start over. I know I screwed up—"

"You weren't the only one," she said.

"Either way, I want a second chance. A real one. Not one where we just try to become friends, but the whole shebang," he said.

She didn't say anything but just stood there with her arms around her waist. In a pair of faded jeans and a T-shirt, she looked lost and confused to him.

Damn.

Maybe his timing was off again. Should he have kept quiet and then…what? He wasn't subtle. He never had been. He was blunt and quick to say what was on his mind.

"Sorry if that isn't what you want to hear, but I'm tired of pretending I don't want you. I was doing an okay job of it until we slept together, and that night made me realize what was important…and it's you."

She nodded.

"Stop nodding and say something. Tell me to go to hell or you need time to think or you're relieved that you're not—"

She closed the distance between them and put her fingers over his lips to stop him from talking. "Enough options. I'm sad because a baby would have been something special we had between us, even if we never figure out how to make a relationship work. I'm confused because part of me wants what you want but another part of me isn't sure we can do it. And because I'm already sad that makes me more hesitant."

He kissed her fingers before drawing her hand into his and leading her over to the bed. He sat on the edge and drew her down on his lap. She easily sat on it and he held her like she was his. And for a moment everything was clear to him.

It was just Hadley and him. That was all he needed in this moment. It might change at some other time but right now it was all about her.

She cuddled closer to him and he held her tight. There was nothing sexual in the moment and she wasn't making him laugh or doing anything to make him feel like a man, but he didn't need that. He simply needed to be here for her and he knew that he was.

He finally knew what she needed from him.

He was realistic enough to know this moment wasn't going to last forever but right now with her in his arms, it was enough.

He was enough.

And that tight knot that he'd felt lately when he was around Hadley completely melted away. He just held her close, rubbing his hand up and down her back. She rested her head right over his heart and he knew that this was what he wanted.

He wanted to find a way to do this.

To be what she needed because it made something inside of him that had always been empty feel sort of full. Not like that aching knot that he usually carried around.

Eventually they ended up lying back on the bed,

her cuddled against his side, and realized that she was spent. He used his smartwatch to turn on some music, the soundtrack from an old movie that she liked, and held her until she went to sleep.

As he watched over her, he knew that Hadley's not being pregnant was probably about the best damned thing to ever happen because now he had a chance to do things right this time. To woo her as a man and not as a frat boy. And that was exactly what he was going to do.

He could be subtle. It would be hard, but he would do it.

For her.

And for him. Because the old Mo had been out of control and it was time to grow up and start adulting for real.

Eleven

One week later, Hadley walked into the Jaqs Veerland Bridal Studio just off Main Street fifteen minutes before she was due to meet her mother and Kinley. She wanted to apologize to Kinley for her mother's autocratic behavior and hang out for a bit before they got down to business.

"Hello?" she called out. The door was open and some soothing Mozart was playing in the background. Hadley drifted over to the portraits of brides and bridal parties that hung on the wall. She recognized a lot of the famous A-list clients but also the locals. Ferrin Caruthers looked absolutely stunning in her simple and elegant Givenchy dress, which had caused a stir when she'd worn it at her wedding. It was all anyone had been able to talk about around town.

She glanced around. It was odd that Kinley hadn't come out to welcome her. The shop usually had an assistant during busy times, but it felt like it was completely abandoned.

Hadley moved toward the private hallway that led to the offices and heard the sound of someone throwing up.

She ran down the hall, stopping at the open bathroom door just as Kinley stood up and groaned.

"You okay?"

Kinley nodded and went to the sink to rinse her mouth out and wipe her face. Hadley handed her one of the monogramed towels that was in the handbasket and then stood back while Kinley composed herself.

"Please don't mention this to anyone," Kinley said when she turned around.

"I won't… I'm guessing you're pregnant?"

"Yes. Nate has been on me to have another kid and even got Penny in on it. At first I was hesitant because of our history, you know?" Kinley said as she opened one of the drawers in the cabinet next to the porcelain washbasin, took out a cosmetic bag and touched up her makeup. Kinley and Nate had first met on a wild weekend in Vegas. After he'd gone back home she found out she was pregnant, and he didn't find out until she came back to Cole's Hill for her job—with the child.

"I do know," Hadley said, thinking about Mo and her, and how she'd sort of wanted a baby but was also very relieved when she found out she wasn't pregnant.

"How did you handle it the first time on your own? I mean that had to have been hard."

"I had no choice. And this time I wanted it to be perfect."

"Isn't it?"

"Well, Penny is going through a new phase and really testing our temper. Nate's trying to be the doting daddy, but he also doesn't want us to raise a brat. In the middle of all this, I went off the Pill without telling him because I thought it'd be a nice surprise, but then last night in bed he let it drop that he thought it was good we only had one kid because they're a lot of work…"

Hadley walked over and hugged her friend. "Worst timing ever. Men are so good at that."

Kinley nodded. "They are. The thing is, I know it's a phase and he'll be back to pestering me about having another one in a week or something, but it did drive home how much work it is and it never seems to get easier. I mean, I thought once Penny could walk and pee by herself I had the motherhood thing in the bag, but it's always something new."

Hadley hadn't even considered any of the things that Kinley was talking about when she'd thought about being pregnant and having a child. She'd thought it might bring her and Mo closer but now it sounded like that might not be the case.

"I had no idea parenting was that hard," Hadley said.

"It's also the best damned thing that ever happened to me. I was a straight up mess before I had Penny and I'd probably still be partying and moving from job to job if I didn't have her. But enough about me. Why are you here early?"

Hadley took a deep breath and looked into the mirror to make sure she didn't have lipstick on her teeth. "I came early to apologize for my mom. She's going to be difficult today."

"It's not like I haven't experienced mothers of the bride before," Kinley said. "I can handle her. My mother might not be Texas-raised but she knew enough about Southern charm to teach me how to deal with the good women of Cole's Hill."

Hadley shook her head. "You're going to need all that learning today. She called your boss on Monday and wants to conference her in on this meeting."

Kinley just smiled as both women left the bathroom and went down the hall to the bridal showroom. "Oh, I know about that. Jaqs is going to be at the meeting this morning. I asked her to come."

Hadley couldn't help but laugh at that. Kinley did indeed know how to handle the women of Cole's Hill. Marrying into one of the Five Families meant she had to deal with them on a daily basis. Her family weren't part of the original five who founded the town but her mom was part of Cole's Hill society so she knew all about the importance the townspeople placed on status.

"Nicely played," Hadley said.

"Like you mentioned, I have to be able to hold my own and I knew she was going to demand to speak to my boss so I saved her the hassle. Also, Jaqs gets off on going toe-to-toe with the *tough cases* as she calls them. Between the two of us, we will make sure she gets everything she wants from the meeting."

Hadley was impressed that her friend was ready to do whatever it took, but then she guessed that was why Kinley and Jaqs were so successful. "I way underestimated you."

"Happens all the time," Kinley said with a wink. "Want a coffee while you wait? Jaqs ordered a new machine and I'm dying for someone to try it out since I'm not having caffeine while I'm preggers."

"Sure."

Hadley watched her friend as she left the showroom and went to make the coffee. Today had been a revelation on a couple of levels. She realized that when she was at home, she fell back into the behavior of a good Cole's Hill daughter. Talking to Kinley this morning had reminded her that she had been also a total badass when she was in Manhattan and she needed to find a way to blend those two personas.

Mauricio started the morning with a run and then headed into the office. When he got there, he was surprised to see Malcolm waiting by the front door. He was kind of slouched over and leaning against the building. When he got closer, it was plain to see his friend was sleeping standing up.

He looked like a mess but didn't smell of booze.

"Malcolm."

His friend's head lolled to one side, and when he

looked up, Mauricio could see his eyes were blood-shot and there was a cut on his cheekbone.

"Dude, are you okay?"

"Yeah…"

Then Malcolm shook his head as he stood up. "Fuck. I'm not. I thought I could handle this but everything is spiraling out of control."

Mauricio squeezed his friend's shoulder. "Let's get out of here. You need breakfast and a shower and then we can talk and figure this out."

For a split second it looked like Malcolm was going to argue but he just conceded, showing none of his usual determined spirit. That worried Mauricio. He led him to his sports car, and once Malcolm was seated, he drove toward Arbol Verde. His brother Diego lived there but he was in London with his wife for the next few weeks, and Mauricio had the feeling that getting out of town would be good for Malcolm.

His friend drifted off as Mauricio drove to the ranch. When they arrived, he parked the car, texted his assistant and told him that he and Malcolm were taking the day off, and then woke his friend and directed him to the guesthouse where he'd be able to shower and change into some clean clothes.

Diego's housekeeper was visiting her family in Dallas while he was gone, so Mo had the place to himself as he went to make breakfast in the main ranch house. He texted Diego to let him know he'd come out to check on the place, something that Mo had promised to do, and that he and Malcolm were going to take a couple of horses for a ride.

His brother called instead of texting back.

"What's up? Why are you at my place on a work-day? Is anything wrong?" Diego asked in that spit-fire way of his.

"Mal is in a bad place. I figured riding would help him sort some stuff out. Otherwise, things are fine here," Mauricio said. "How's London?"

"Cold and wet," Diego said. "But Pippa is launch-ing her new product line of Classic H jewelry for House of Hamilton on Friday and she's so excited that the weather doesn't matter."

"Of course, it doesn't. When your woman is happy, all is right in the world," Mauricio said. He wished that he'd learned that lesson a bit sooner. Maybe then he wouldn't have to work so hard to get Hadley back.

"That sounds very mature coming from you. Are you back with Hadley?" Diego asked.

"We're still working that out," he said. "But I'm hopeful this time I won't screw it up."

"You're too hard on yourself," Diego said. "Sure, you've had some issues, but you always owned them."

He tried. But there had been times in the past when he felt like all he did was fail. "Thank you for say-ing that."

"That's what big brothers are for," Diego said. "I'll be home this weekend for the polo match. I'd like to make this an annual event."

"I've been doing some work around that," Mau-ricio said, then caught his brother up on the corpo-rate sponsors he'd reached out to. A lot of them he worked with in conjunction with his housing charity work. Diego was impressed and Mo, who'd always been happy being the hothead, realized that he liked getting attention for doing something that was good. He liked not always being the brother who was in hot water. He thought that was Hadley's influence and he realized how much she was changing him…or maybe helping him to change. He doubted she'd even realize just how much she had.

"See you on Friday, Mo," Diego said. "Love ya."

"Love ya too," he said ending the call as Mal walked into the breakfast room.

His friend still looked like crap but his eyes were clearer.

"Are you using?" Mo asked without preamble.

It was the only thing he could think of that could explain how messed up Mal looked and the money that had disappeared from the wedding account he and Helena had set up.

"No. I'm not. Why do you think that?"

"You look like shit, you still haven't paid back your wedding account, your fiancée is freaked and you aren't manning up. Something is definitely up with you. And I'm not about to go all Dr. Phil but you need to fess up and get straight."

Mal turned one of the breakfast chairs around and straddled it. He put his elbows on the ladderback and his head in his hands. "God, when you say it like that I can see how out of control my life has gotten."

"Yes, it has. So what the hell is going on?"

Mal rubbed the back of his neck but still wouldn't look Mo in the eyes. He honestly feared for his friend.

This wasn't the man he'd known. This person was evasive and there was something, almost a desperation to him.

"I can't…"

"Just say it. You know I'm going to find out," Mauricio said. "You were the one who found me at the Bull Pit and told me if I got into one more fight, Sheriff Justiss was going to put me in jail on a thirty-day hold. You said *don't screw your life up*."

"I did say that," Mal said, looking him in the eye for the first time in weeks. "I guess it's easier to give advice when you see your best friend crash and burn than to take it yourself."

"Definitely. I thought drinking and fighting was the way to get over Hadley, but it wasn't. And I don't even know what demon you're battling."

He put a mug of black coffee and a plate of food in front of his friend before sitting down across from him.

"It sounds stupid when I say it out loud," Mal said.

"Fair enough, since you've been acting like an ass."

His friend gave him a faint smile. "I started thinking about the future. My in-laws have a really nice life and I knew I had to provide at least that level of comfort for Helena. And you know me. I work hard, but I play hard too."

"Nothing wrong with that. Helena loves you, not your money."

"You think?"

"Of course! It's an insult to Helena and yourself if

you think otherwise. If she wanted a trust-fund man, she could have found one. She loves you."

Mal rubbed the back of his neck. "Well, I had a line on a sure-thing bet that would double our wedding fund and give her the extras she'd been scrimping on so I took the money and placed the bet…"

"And lost," Mauricio said. "Who did you gamble with?"

"No one you know. Anyway, I've been working extra hard to try to make back the money, but we saved for two years to afford our wedding and I lost the money in one night… I mean, if I lost it in one night—"

"No. Stop. You're never going to win it back like that. Damn. Why didn't you come to me?"

"Why would I? This is my problem," Mal said.

"Well, screw you too. I thought we were friends."

"Sorry, Mo. I didn't think of it that way. I just was damned mad at myself. I don't know how to get out of this. I've been working odd jobs around the area—not in Cole's Hill—to try to make up the money. I told Helena I'd get it back in our wedding account before we had to make all the payments, but I'm not sure I can," Malcolm said, pushing his plate away. He stood up and walked over to the French doors, putting his hands on his hips and staring out at the rolling hills.

"I'll help you. Alec is really good at investing and together the three of us can figure out a way that doesn't involve gambling to get your money back."

"Really?"

"Hell, yes. But you have to do something first," Mauricio said.

"What?"

"Come clean with Helena. She's freaked out, and I think only by being honest will you be able to fix this. She needs to know what's in your head and your heart."

"I thought you weren't going to go all Dr. Phil," Malcolm said wryly.

"I can't help it. I'm the wisest of our group."

"You keep telling yourself that," Malcolm said with a bit of humor in his voice.

Mo felt like he was seeing his old friend come through for the first time since the engagement party.

Mal reached over and awkwardly hugged him. "Thank you."

"No problem. You call Helena. I'm going to text Alec and maybe we can get something going with your investments."

Thirty minutes later Helena was at the Arbol Verde. Mauricio stayed in the house while his friends went for a horseback ride.

Helena had been surprised to get the call from Malcolm. He hadn't been home in two days and she hadn't slept in that time. She was worried, angry and edgy. Her mom was in a power play with Jaqs Veerland, and honestly at this point she wasn't sure she even wanted to get married. But there was no way she was backing out of the wedding of the year unless she was sure that Malcolm was truly gone.

So this call… Well, it was exactly what she'd been both hoping for and dreading. Whatever was going on with him, it sounded like he was going to come clean. She hoped it wasn't another woman. She knew she wouldn't be able to handle that. Or at least she thought she wouldn't.

"You haven't said a word since we left the barn," Malcolm said.

She wasn't going to lie, she was afraid to start this conversation. She shook her head. She was the strong sister, the one everyone could pile stuff on and she'd deal with it, but here she was riding next to Mal, pretending he didn't look like hell. None of it made sense. The knot in her gut got tighter.

"I don't know what to say. I'm scared," she said, pushing her sunglasses up on her head and glancing over at him. He had on a straw cowboy hat and dark glasses so his face was pretty much hidden from her. But she'd seen his bloodshot eyes earlier.

"I'm sorry, Hel. I never meant to do this to you," he said.

"What have you done? I mean, I know the money is missing. Is it gone? What did you do with it?" she asked.

He pulled his horse to a stop and dismounted. She did the same. The horses at Arbol Verde were trained to stay when their leads were on the ground so she dropped them and went over to him.

Suddenly all the anger she'd been pushing down since she'd first seen that low balance in their account exploded and she couldn't help it—she shoved him hard on the shoulder. "What the hell are you doing? If you don't want to get married, just say that. Don't dick around and screw up everything so I'm the one who has to be the adult and break things off. You were never a douchebag before."

He stood there and let her rant at him, which made her stop. She hated losing her cool, so she stepped back, wrapping her arms around her waist, and just waited.

"I'm sorry. That wasn't ladylike."

"I deserve it," he said. "The truth is, I know I'm not the man your family wishes you'd fallen for. I can't keep you in the same style as your parents. I saw a chance to change that, to give you what you needed and it didn't work out."

"What I needed? Let's deal with that BS first. When have I ever said I needed more than you?" she asked. She wasn't going to be able to keep her cool, especially if he was trying to play this like it was all her fault.

"Never. You've never made me feel like I wasn't enough. But you are… Well, you are my heart, Helena, and I want to give you the world, but I can't. And I wanted more for you and for me. For us," he said.

Damn.

Of course, he wasn't making it about her. Malcolm always had big dreams and a big heart, which was why she'd fallen for him. "I don't need more. We don't. What did you do?"

He sighed, shoving his hands through his hair,

which knocked the cowboy hat to the ground. They both ignored it.

"I took our money and placed a very large bet on a sure thing and lost it all," he said. "I've been trying to get the money back—"

"By gambling?"

"No. Not that. I don't have a large enough stake to make it work," he said. "I've been doing odd jobs all over the county, working nights to try to get some of it back."

"Malcolm, you should have said."

"I couldn't. I felt dumb enough that I lost all of our wedding money and then you had to go to your parents, which I know you didn't want to do," he said. "And I made the mess so I had to fix it."

She walked over to him and wrapped her arms around him. He hugged her close and the tension in her stomach started to disappear. "We can fix this. We're partners for life, Mal. We can do this together. The money doesn't matter as long as we are together."

"I love you," Malcolm said.

"I love you too."

He told her about reaching out to Mauricio and how they had a plan to consult with Alec and invest the money to rebuild the funds from the wedding account. Helena offered her advice, but she knew that Alec was better with investments than she was. She felt like they were on the right track. She knew that all couples had tough times and maybe they were having theirs now so that they'd be stronger once they were married.

Twelve

When Hadley arrived at the large Five Families mansion where Mo's parents lived, she stood outside for a moment and reflected. Going to a polo match brought back so many memories of her relationship with Mauricio. Now his mother was hosting a brunch before the game and, of course, all of the extended Velasquez family would be there. Hadley wondered if she was really doing this, if she was really going to jump back into a life with him.

But the last few weeks had been…well, what she'd always hoped things could be between them. While there were still some areas that neither of them seemed to want to delve into, she did feel that this time they were making changes that would make them stronger as a couple.

"Nervous?" Mo asked, coming up beside her and putting his hand on the small of her back. A shiver went down her spine, making her wish they'd made love one more time before they came here.

"Yes. Your mom never thought I was good enough for you, and when we broke up, she probably was very happy."

Mo leaned down and kissed her. It was one of those deep passionate kisses of his that made her feel like she was going to melt into a puddle at his feet. This was exactly why she'd been struggling to believe that they were real. This incendiary passion that always exploded between them felt like an addiction, one that would leave her strung out if she couldn't get her daily hit of him. Actually, she knew what that felt like.

The stakes were higher this time. She knew that if they couldn't make this work, he'd be gone from her life forever. They were both too smart to keep hitting their heads against the wall.

"She thought *I* wasn't good enough for *you*," he corrected, as he lifted his head and brushed a strand of hair behind her ear. "She knew you'd hurt me when you finally realized it."

She shook her head. "Did I hurt you?"

"I got drunk for three months and then started fights with every guy you tried to date… What do you think?"

"That you don't like to lose," she admitted.

He shook his head. Wrapping both arms around her, he pulled her close in a tight bear hug and leaned down, whispering into her ear, "I never thought I could hurt like I did when we were apart, darling. I never want to feel that way again."

She hugged him back, twisting her head so that she could rest her cheek on his shoulder. "Me neither."

"Yo, bro, maybe save the making out for when you're alone. Mom definitely doesn't approve of PDA."

Hadley lifted her head and stepped back as Alec came up the walk.

Mo shot him the bird, then draped his arm around Hadley's shoulder and turned to walk toward the front door with his twin following them. Her nerves were gone as she entered the house, giving her handbag to the Velasquez family butler and following Mo into the drawing room where they were announced.

Mrs. Velasquez was deep in conversation with her group of friends. Diego called Mauricio over to the group of men Hadley recognized from pictures on the polo club walls. These were the other investors in the new development, some of them world famous players and horse breeders.

She excused herself, knowing that she didn't want to be the only woman in a group of men talking about horses, and made her way down the hall toward the living room. The door to the hall bathroom opened as she walked by and Bianca stepped out with her young son, Benito. He was dressed in jodhpurs, riding boots and a polo shirt. He smiled when he saw her.

"*Buenos días*, Hadley."

"Hiya, Benito. Are you riding today?"

"*Si*, during the… What's it called, Mama?"

"He is going to be riding with Diego during an exhibition," Bianca said. Bianca was several months pregnant and glowed with an inner beauty. But she also looked a bit tired.

"That sounds like fun. Want to tell me all about it?" she asked the little boy. She'd known him since he was born, and as he tucked his tiny hand into hers, she realized how intertwined her life and Mauricio's were and how much she'd missed his family.

She followed the pair back down the hall toward the backyard where the brunch had been set up. Everyone else had come out from the living room. She stood there to the side for a short time, just watching Mo with his family, and she couldn't help noticing that he seemed way more relaxed than he'd been in a long time.

When someone came up beside her, she glanced over to see it was his mother. "I didn't think you'd give him another chance."

"I… We…"

"It's okay. I know that love is complicated. I've been married to Mauricio's father for a long time and it still isn't easy. I'm glad to see you with him. He's different now. More relaxed with everyone. I like it."

"Me too," Hadley said.

"Come on, let's have a Texas Sunrise cocktail and join the men," Mrs. Velasquez said, and just like that Hadley felt like she was part of the family. Part of this group that she'd wanted to be a part of ever since she and Mo had first started dating. But she'd always been trying to be perfect, trying to prove to herself and to everyone else that she and Mauricio were the perfect couple. It had never been real, and had put distance between her and Mo's family.

As she followed his mother and joined him, she knew that this time Mauricio wasn't the only who was different. She was too. It was humbling to realize that she hadn't been as mature as she'd always thought she was.

When she got to Mo, he leaned down to kiss her cheek and whispered, "See, I told you she liked you."

She just laughed and shook her head.

Mauricio was tired by the time the charity polo match was over. But he knew that this was what he wanted. He was grateful that Malcolm had shown up for the game and had played well. Even Helena was there, standing next to Hadley in the viewing area and cheering them both on. He couldn't help but think that as the hashtags on Instagram always put it, he was living his best life in this moment.

That thought made him feel anxious, like a major screwup was just around the corner, and he knew that was because in the past he'd never been able to simply let himself be content. Part of it was that he'd always been hungry for more, trying to fill that emptiness deep inside of him with something, but never really finding the right thing.

Hadley… Well, he hoped she was it, but he knew it was dangerous to put that on her. The fact was he had to be content in himself before he could be totally committed to their relationship. If helping Malcolm deal with his own shit had shown him anything, it was that very fact.

Malcolm was running and trying to do something to impress his fiancée instead of realizing that he was enough for Helena.

Mauricio had to wonder if he was enough for Hadley. That was always the question, and it had never been answered between them. They both had spent a lot of time looking outside of the relationship, but that pregnancy scare had bonded them, made them a team. Since that moment he'd felt like…well, almost like they were a couple once more.

He rubbed the back of his neck. Okay, he was overthinking this. But he didn't want to lose her again. He didn't want to jeopardize the second chance he still wasn't sure he deserved but that he wanted more than anything.

He showered and changed and met up with Alec. "I forgot how much I like playing."

"I know. When we were kids I always resented being forced outside to ride and practice polo with Dad but now, I'm glad I was," his brother said.

"No one would have believed we were twins if you'd stayed inside… You were getting too nerdy."

"Nerdy? You wish, bro. Women like my smarts," Alec said.

"Is that what they tell you?"

"Trust me. I know they do."

"What do you know?" Hadley asked as they approached her.

"That brains are sexier than brawn," Alec said.

"Good thing Mo has both," she said with a wink that sent a shot of pure desire straight through him.

"You think so? He's not as smart as me."

"No one is as smart as you," she said.

"True," Alec said.

When Alec drifted over to the bar, Mo stood there in front of Hadley, realizing how much he wanted her to be right here by his side for the rest of his life. But he couldn't say that. They were taking it slow, not making the same mistakes again. But there was a part of him that was afraid to pump the brakes. He had that feeling…the one that told him to grab her with both hands before he lost her again.

"You were pretty impressive today," she said, after Alec had left.

No doubt his brother was going to try to woo some women. Alec had been different lately, and it was only now that Mauricio was noticing it because he'd been busy trying to keep Malcolm from imploding and losing the only woman he'd ever loved.

"Thanks. I try," he said wryly. "I noticed Helena was with you earlier. Where did she go?"

"To find Malcolm. She told me what you did for him. Well, for them. That was really nice," she said.

"Thanks," he replied. He watched as she looked around at the crowd.

"Being here is strange," she finally said. "I mean, this is the first time we are together with our families. Your mom was nice earlier. Helena commented that she was glad we were back together. But this involves our families and friends, and that scares me."

He pulled her into a quiet corner and turned so she was blocked from everyone's view by his body. He looked down into her brown eyes that always hid her real thoughts and feelings from him, but in this moment, he had no doubt what she was thinking. She was nervous just as he was, afraid that now that they'd gone public with this second chance that everyone would be second-guessing them.

"I don't care what anyone else thinks about us," he said, realizing that it was the truth. "You're the only one I care about."

"Mo."

She just said his name but there was so much in that one word. So much emotion. She was trying to make sense of this the same way he was.

"We got this, darling. I'm not going to let any outside pressure contribute to bringing us down. Not this time. If the past has taught me anything, it's that I'm much better with you by my side."

She tipped her head to the side, studying him in a way that made him realize how vulnerable he was to her. He stood a bit straighter, knowing he wanted her to see whatever it was she was searching for.

"I am too," she said at last.

She leaned up to wrap her hands around his shoulders and kissed him, and in that moment, he realized that if he lost her this time, he might not recover. That Hadley had somehow made her way into that empty part of his soul that he'd never realized had been waiting for her to fill it.

* * *

Helena left the others and went to find Malcolm. Mauricio had been a godsend in helping her figure out something was wrong with her fiancé. But she still wasn't sure if the problem was fully solved. Did Malcolm have a gambling problem?

Or was it what he'd told her—that he just wanted to give her a good life? As if they didn't already have one. After meeting him at Arbol Verde, she'd taken him back home with her and they'd had a good long talk. Today was the first time since the engagement party when she'd realized the money was missing that she felt like things were back to normal. But a doubt still nagged at the back of her mind.

Malcolm was talking to Diego and Alec, and she saw how relaxed he looked. It gave her hope that they were finally over the rough patch that had threatened their marriage.

"Hey, Hel, you okay?" Hadley asked as she slipped her arm around Helena's shoulders.

"Yeah, I think I am," she said, sneaking a cocktail off the tray of a passing waiter while her sister did the same. "Love is so dammed complicated, you know?"

Hadley nodded and then took a sip of her drink. "Wouldn't it be nice if it were like those stories we read as teenagers, and once the girl fell for the guy all the problems sort of magically disappeared?"

Helena had to smile at her sister. "Yes. Especially when I'm in the middle of planning a wedding. I used to think there was no difference in living together and being married, but honestly, knowing that we're going to be a couple for the rest of our lives is enough to freak me out sometimes. I get that it could do the same to Mal, but there are moments when I still can't figure out why he can't just…"

"It's okay," she said. "We're allowed to expect the men in our lives to step up when we need them to."

"Is that what's going on with you and Mauricio now? Is he stepping up?"

Hadley chewed her lower lip and looked across the room at him as he talked to his parents and someone Helena didn't know.

"Yes, I think so. We've been dating—well, hooking up for the last couple of weeks—and this is the first time we're out as a couple. It's scary and exciting. How can it be both of those things?"

"I don't know. But I get it. So, you've been hooking up?"

"He's the one guy I can't get over," Hadley admitted. "Even when I was dating other guys, I always compared them to Mo. I thought that was crazy until I realized that there was something between us that I couldn't explain and now… Well, I think we're both really committed this time."

Helena wrapped her arm around her sister's waist. "Good. I'm glad to hear that. I think you both needed to grow up a bit."

"Of course, you did," Hadley said, pulling away. "It's not like you and Mal are any more normal than we are."

"Don't I know it. Maybe we are all just bumbling along," Helena said.

"Yeah, I think we are," she said, then groaned. Helena followed her sister's gaze and noticed her mom was walking toward them.

"I thought Mom was going to lose it the other day before Jaqs walked into the meeting," Helena said.

"I did too. She really wants your wedding to be perfect," Hadley said. "I don't know if perfect is ever possible though."

"Of course it is," their mother said as she joined them. "You two look beautiful today."

"Thanks, Mom," Helena and Hadley said at the same time. Their mother seemed more chill today than she had been at the last meeting with the wedding planner, and maybe that was because Helena was more at ease, as well.

She hadn't wanted to tell her mom about any of her problems with Malcolm, but Helena knew she'd been broadcasting her worries by her behavior and it hadn't made the wedding planning sessions with Kinley any easier.

"Both of your men played well today," Mom said.

"They did," Helena said.

"Are you okay with me and Mo?" Hadley asked, sounding a little nervous.

Her mom reached out, tucking the strand of Hadley's hair that always wanted to be free back behind her ear. "If you are."

"Really?" Helena asked.

"Yes. You girls think I have some dream guy in mind for you both and the truth is, I do. I want a man you love, a man who loves you and treats you right.

That's it. Malcolm makes you happier than I have ever seen you before, Helena. And for some reason, Hadley, Mauricio is the one guy you have never been able to walk away from."

Helena glanced at Hadley and easily read the surprise on her face. Their mom had been vocal and judgy about every guy they brought home in the past.

"What brought on this change?"

"Something your father said to me the other day," Mom said.

"What was that?" Helena asked. Daddy did have a way of making Mom see sense and not act like the queen of the world.

"Just that you girls wanted something different from life than I did. And he told me to stop trying to force my ideals on you," Mom said. "He had a point. I want you to have the man of your dreams, not the guy I imagine you'd like."

Helena reached over and hugged her mother and Hadley did the same. It made her realize that love was always complicated, even when it was between a parent and child.

Malcolm and Mauricio joined them, and for a moment Helena felt like everything was perfect in her world. She was happy with the man she loved, and her baby sister had finally figured out how to make things work with the man she wanted.

Thirteen

The text message from her client in New York wasn't one she was looking forward to reading. The client had exacting standards, and like her mom always said, if someone was paying for something, they wanted it to be the best. But Hadley felt like no matter what she did, it was never good enough for this client.

"You're frowning at your phone," Mauricio said.

"I know. It's an email from Jenner," she admitted to him. They were sprawled on her couch. Mo had put the Spurs game on and she was sitting with her feet in his lap, alternating between looking at her email and checking out bridesmaids dress designs on the private website Kinley had sent her.

"Isn't that job over?"

"I thought so, but this email means he probably

needs one more tweak to his marketing campaign, which I designed."

"You'll never know if you don't open it up."

She stuck her tongue out at him. "You don't say."

"Open it. Whatever it is, not knowing is worse than whatever he wants. Plus, I don't want it to ruin our entire Sunday."

She leaned her head back against the couch and studied him. They had spent the entire weekend together and she was starting to get used to living with him. Everything was different this time. He was different. Before he would have been on his phone or taking calls or rushing out to meet a potential buyer. Instead, he'd been dedicated to making this time together quality time.

She tossed her phone on the coffee table and straddled his lap.

He pushed his hands up under her T-shirt and with the snap of his fingers undid the clasp of her bra.

"Do that thing you do," he said.

She quirked her head to the side. "What thing?"

"That thing where you take your bra off without removing your shirt," he said, his voice dropping a decibel and rumbling through her, turning her on.

She reached under the sleeves of her T-shirt, slowly drawing the bra strap down her left arm, taking her time as she pulled her hand from underneath the elastic. He was watching her as if she were performing some sort of complicated task and it made her smile. She loved seeing him so serious about her. She slowly drew the second strap down her other arm and then tugged her lace bra out of the sleeve and dropped it on his chest.

"Was it as good as you remembered?" she asked, arching one eyebrow at him.

"Better," he said, putting his hands on her waist and then pulling the hem of her T-shirt until it was tight against her body. "That's what I wanted to see."

She glanced down at her chest and saw that he'd made it so her light colored T-shirt was pressed against her chest and her nipples were visible through it.

She put her hands on his shoulders, kneading them as she shifted on his thighs, pushing her shoulders back so that her breasts were thrust toward him.

"Are you just looking tonight?"

He made a sort of rumbling noise that didn't really answer her question, but then she felt his arm moving up behind her back, holding her as his head came forward. She felt the heat of his breath on her nipple before his mouth closed over it, sucking her through the fabric of her shirt.

She closed her eyes and let her head fall back, pushing her fingers into his hair and holding him. But then he lifted his head, moving to her other breast and doing the same thing to her other nipple.

The wet fabric clung to her skin and she shivered. He shifted back, undoing the button fly of his jeans, and she glanced down to see the firm ridge of his cock pressing against the fabric of his boxer briefs. She reached down to stroke him, and he smiled as she ran her hand up and down his length, feeling him grow underneath her touch.

"That's better," he said.

She leaned over him, using the hand that was in his hair to urge his head back as she brought her mouth down on his. He opened his lips under hers, his tongue thrusting up into her mouth, and she couldn't help but bite it. He turned her on like no one else, and though she'd started out with a slow burn in mind, there was no way that was going to happen with him now.

She pushed herself off his lap and stood next to him, watching as he pushed his underwear down to free himself. Then he took his length in his fist, stroking up and down.

She melted a little and shifted her legs. He watched her with narrowed eyes as she slowly undid the buttons on her jeans and lowered them down her legs, swiveling her hips and thrusting her breasts forward as she did so. She paused and looked up at him when her jeans were at her knees. He stared at her pointed nipples, then his gaze slowly moved down to her white lace bikini panties.

"Like what you see?"

"You know I do," he said. "I wouldn't mind seeing you disrobe from the other side."

To be honest, she knew that. Mauricio liked her butt. It wasn't as though she was extra curvy or anything, but he liked the way she looked from all sides. He'd told her more than once, and tonight, with the new knowledge that they were stronger as a couple, she wanted to make this hotter than it had ever been before.

She turned around and slowly drew one leg from her jeans and then the other. As she stepped out of them, she bent over so he could see her backside and glanced at him over her shoulder. His cock had gotten so hard that she was pretty sure it wouldn't take much to push him over the edge. And that was exactly what she wanted.

She wanted him so on fire for her that he forgot the past and the future, and thought of nothing but the two of them in this moment.

She turned around and pulled at the hem of her shirt, slowly pulling it up over her head. As she tossed it aside, she felt his hands on her breasts and his thigh between hers. He rubbed his leg against her center and she arched her back, feeling one of his hands move around to hold her to him.

She let her head fall back, trusting him to hold her up. His mouth was on her breast and his other hand slowly moved down her body, tracing her ribs, then dipping into her belly button and then lower, skirting over the top of her mound. He palmed her, rubbing his hand over her, and then slowly she felt his fingers parting her.

She reached for him. Taking his long length in her hand, she stroked him up and down, and she used her grip on his cock to rub the tip of it against her clit. It felt so good, pulses of pleasure rushed through her.

He bit her nipple lightly and then he fell back on the couch with a bounce. He maneuvered her until she lay on the sofa cushions and he came down over her. She rubbed his chest; he was still wearing his shirt.

"Mauricio," she said.

"Yes, darling," he responded.

"Why are you still wearing your shirt?" she asked.

"You like it," he said.

"I like it when I can feel your skin better," she said.

The soft sound of her voice, the teasing tone and husky timbre, inflamed him and made it hard for him to think about anything other than driving his cock deep inside of her and taking her over and over again until they were both exhausted. This was what Sundays were made for, he thought. Making love to Hadley.

He took her hand in his and kissed it before bringing it to the buttons on his shirt. She slowly undid them. He held himself over her body. Each brush of her fingers against his skin drove him closer to the edge, to the moment when all this teasing was going to be too much and he was going to just thrust up into her. Hell, he didn't even care that his condoms were in her bedroom.

But he knew he should. They were rebuilding their trust and he couldn't expect her to trust him if he didn't use protection.

"Dammit. The condoms are in your room," he said.

"Then take me there," she said.

"Wrap your legs and arms around me," he said.

She did, her center pressed against him and her

breasts against his chest, her arms underneath his shirt holding him tightly to her.

He groaned, knowing if he shifted his hips the tiniest bit, he could enter her. But he didn't. He sat up and pulled her close to him with one hand as he stood up and walked across her loft to her bedroom, not stopping until he reached the bed. He sat down on it and she straddled him, dropping a kiss on his mouth that made him harder than he'd been before.

She shifted, her breasts brushing against his chest as she reached for the nightstand and the box of condoms he'd put there earlier. She grabbed the box and handed it to him.

His entire body felt too hot. Like he was going to explode if he didn't get inside her. But he shoved his own need down. He didn't want to waste a moment of this second chance with her. Putting his hand on her waist, he felt her brush over his erection. Her nipples were beaded and hard.

She arched her back, which thrust her breasts forward, and a growl escaped him. He put his hands on her waist as she leaned forward, the tips of her breasts grazing his chest. Her mouth was on his neck, kissing and nibbling up the length of it until she reached his ear. Scraping her teeth down the column of his neck, she suckled the pulse that beat there and then lightly bit his skin.

He groaned, "Woman, I can't take much more."

"Good."

He shifted his hips to rub the ridge of his erection against her center.

She bit him again with a little more force and then shifted back to put her hand between their bodies, rubbing his cock.

She scratched his chest with her nail, tracing the thin line of hair that ran down to his stomach and lower. He shuddered. He wasn't going to make it much longer. He brought his hand to hers and held her hand to his pecs for a moment, placing it over his heart. It was then that he realized how much she meant to him. That this was more than he'd expected to find with any woman. He wished he could tell her, but he didn't have the words and he wasn't sure she'd believe him.

"Hadley."

"Don't," she said, putting her finger on his lips. "Don't talk. Just take me, Mo. Make me forget everything but you."

He nodded. He wanted her and in this moment that was all that mattered. Her other hand was on his erection, rubbing him, and he shifted his legs. His mind was no longer on talking; it was on her sex. He needed her naked.

He needed to be buried inside her. Talking could wait for later. He lowered his mouth to hers. Her lips met his and he thrust his tongue deep inside, taking her the way he wanted to take her.

She sucked on his tongue and drew it deeper into her mouth. He shifted back on the bed until he felt the headboard against his back. Putting her hands on his shoulders, she leaned down and kissed his chest. He saw her tongue dart out and brush his nipple.

She traced each of the muscles that rippled in his abdomen and then slowly made her way lower. His cock was so hard he thought he couldn't get any harder. He felt his heartbeat with each pulse through his shaft. He wanted to take control and get inside of her. But another part of him wanted to just sit back and let her have her way with him.

Her hand went to his erection, brushing over his straining length. He wrapped his arm around her back, holding her so that his forearm was aligned with her spine and he could tunnel his fingers into the back of her hair. Then he brought their chests together so that her nipples were poking his torso.

Blood roared in his ears. He was so hard, so full right now, that he needed her. To claim her. To make it so she never left him again.

Skimming his fingers down her body, he found her center. It was warm and wet and he parted her, tapping her clit lightly. Her hands tightened on his shoulders as she arched her back, her head falling to the side as he rubbed her sensitive flesh.

She bit her lower lip as she shifted her hips, moving until he was touching her in the exact right spot. He wanted more. Needed her to come for him. He slipped one finger lower and traced the opening of her body, and then when she moaned, he pushed two fingers up into her.

He worked his fingers in and out of her, keeping one finger on her clit, rubbing and tapping against her as she began to rock against him with more urgency. She put her hands on either side of his face and drew his mouth to her breast. She brushed her nipple over his mouth and he sucked on it, drew it between his lips and teased the tip with his tongue.

He caressed her, bringing both of his hands down her back until he could cup her ass in his hands.

Then he went back to thrusting his fingers deeper into her. When he felt her body start to tighten around him, he bit her nipple, which pushed her over the edge. She called his name as she came and he held her until she quieted. Then he rolled over so that she was underneath him and he put his hands on her ankles and drew her legs apart, putting one knee on the bed between her spread legs.

He quickly put on a condom before leaning over her, placing his hands on the bed near her breasts, he lowered himself over her and rubbed her body with his, loving the feel of her underneath him. She reached for his cock again and he caught her hand, lacing the fingers of her left hand through his and stretching it over her head. She smiled at him.

He pushed his hips between her thighs and she wrapped her legs around his waist. He felt her hand on the right side of his chest and glanced down to see her tracing his tattoo of his family's crest this time. What did that mean?

But he couldn't think right now. Instead, he drew his hips back and entered her, taking her as deeply as he could. Her hand fell to his shoulder, her nails digging into his skin as he drove himself into her, her head tipping back and her eyes drifting closed with each inch he gave her. She took it all. All of him.

He leaned down and caught one of her nipples in his teeth, scraping it very gently. She started to tighten around him. Her hips were moving faster, demanding more, but he kept the pace slow, steady, wanting her to come before he did.

He suckled her nipple and rotated his hips to catch her pleasure point with each thrust. Her fists were clenching in his hair as she threw her head back and her climax ripped through her.

A moment later he followed her, coming hard and deep and feeling like he'd lost his soul to her. He cradled her close in the aftermath and held her to him. She opened her eyes and looked at him in a way he couldn't explain, and he wanted to believe that something had changed.

They spent the rest of the evening in bed, talking about her job and the fact that she had to go to New York. Mauricio had a pang at the thought of her leaving. He needed her by his side. Something had changed inside of him and he was afraid to say it out loud.

But he needed Hadley more than he had thought he would.

Fourteen

Manhattan wasn't as fun as Hadley remembered. She found the pace dizzying instead of invigorating. She missed her morning coffee from the new shop that had opened in the retail park near her loft and frankly, as she stretched out in the king-sized bed in her friend's guest bedroom, she missed Mauricio. When they'd made love on her couch before she left, she knew something had changed between them. That she was in love with him again. Had she ever really fallen out of love with him?

She was beginning to think she hadn't, but she was definitely in love now. And that scared her. She'd left him more than once and each time it had been harder than she'd ever imagined it could be. And they were back together but trusting him… Well, it was getting easier because he was so different from the man she'd walked in on with another woman. But the truth was, there was always going to be a little part of her that believed that it couldn't last.

She didn't know if it was her past experiences with Mo or her sister being brutally honest about her problems with her fiancé. But something kept Hadley from letting go and just trusting Mauricio fully.

She felt like a mean girl for holding back though. They'd talked on the phone last night until 2:00 a.m. He was in Houston today. He was receiving a charity award at a ceremony later tonight, and he had been cute, trying to say that he didn't deserve the honor. But she had seen firsthand how hard he worked building houses for the underprivileged in Cole's Hill. While the economy of their small town was growing, there were always those who didn't benefit from the new industries, and Mauricio was doing his part to make sure as many families as he could help wouldn't be left behind.

She was proud of him.

She couldn't think of a time in the past when she had felt like that. He'd always been driven by success and trying to become a millionaire before he turned thirty. It was something he'd done many times over at this point, but it had driven him for so long that the man she knew had been lost.

And it made her happy to think that he had changed.

If only she could make herself believe the change was real. Her phone rang, and she glanced over to see it was Mauricio video calling her. She glanced around her friend's apartment to make sure she was alone, that Merri was still in her own room before answering the call. Merri and she had been cubicle mates in the office and after Hadley had gone freelance, Merri always offered her the guest room when she was in the city for business.

"Hey, you," she said as the call connected. She saw he was in the hotel bathroom, fresh from a shower—she could tell because his hair was still damp and he had shaving cream on his face.

"Hey, darling," Mo said, turning to face the screen. "Missed you this morning and thought you could get ready with me."

"I'd love to watch you get ready," she said.

He arched an eyebrow at her. "I was hoping I'd catch you before you were ready for your day, but I can see I'm too late."

"You are," she said. "I got up early to practice my presentation one more time. I think I'm ready."

"I know you are. You'll wow them like you always do," he said, turning away from the camera and leaning toward the mirror to shave. He had a white towel wrapped around his lean hips. She curled her legs underneath her body to watch him. "Thanks for that," she said.

"I set up an alert for Manhattan, Upper East Side, on my phone and there are a few places that might make a nice investment for us," he said.

"Us?"

He stopped shaving and turned to face her. "Isn't there an us?"

She nibbled on her lower lip. All those things she had wanted to say and to hear from him in return before she'd left for New York were coming out in the open now.

"Yes. I want there to be an us. Do you?"

"Had, I'm looking at real estate, so we can have a place to stay when your freelance business takes you to Manhattan," he said. "I thought that would make my intentions clear."

"I need the words, Mo. I need to know what you are thinking," she admitted. "I don't want to guess at what you want and hope that we're both on the same page. I did that before and it backfired."

"Fair enough," he said, rinsing his razor, then turning to face her and leaning toward the camera. "Let me make this clear, I want to share my life with you. Do you want that? Or do you still have doubts about me?"

She smiled, and mimicked his movements and looked straight at him through the phone's camera. "Let me make this clear. I want that too."

He smiled at her, that sweet smile that he saved for only a few people, and she felt her heart beat a little faster. She knew she loved him, but she didn't want to tell him that over a video call.

"Good. Now that we have that settled, should I text you the addresses? You can go by and check them out while you're in town," he said.

"Or we could come back for a weekend trip just for fun and check them out together," she suggested.

"I like that. I'll have my assistant make the travel arrangements. Send me your calendar," he said.

"I will. I think the only major things I have are Helena and Malcolm's pre-wedding stuff. Now that he's back to being normal, it looks like everything is going to move a little more quickly than previously."

"Good. Those two belong together," he said.

"I agree. Thank you for what you did," she said. To be honest, the old Mauricio was more about himself than his friends and his helping Malcolm and pointing him to a smart way to improve his finances had really impressed her. But more than that, she could tell Mauricio had started to look at the world beyond himself. He'd put his friend first and that was something the old Mo wouldn't have done.

That made her heart overflow with love.

Damn.

Love.

She had been pretending the entire time they were dating that she was being smarter this time, that she wouldn't make the same mistake of falling for him until she knew—what? There were no guarantees in love and she knew that if she was going to have any chance at true happiness with Mauricio, she was going to have to trust him and trust herself.

Why was that so hard?

Mo had convinced Alec to come with him to Houston today. The twins were sharing a hotel room, but

Alec planned to skip tonight's Houston Cares humanitarian dinner—it just wasn't his thing. Still, Mo appreciated the company.

Not that long ago he'd have gone by himself and found someone to keep him company after the dinner and the reception. But of course, that was the old Mauricio, one who hadn't realized just how much having the right woman in his world enhanced it. He'd spent a lot of time buying million-dollar houses and selling them, thinking that he would have his own and the perfect woman to be his hostess. But he had never realized that those properties were always going to feel empty without the right woman in them.

"Bro, you look too serious right now. What's on your mind?"

On his mind? He wanted Hadley to be his. Not his girlfriend but his wife. He wanted her by his side as his partner for the rest of his life. And…he wasn't sure she was there yet. That she'd forgiven him for past mistakes and saw the changes he felt he'd made.

"I'm thinking about Hadley. I miss her," he said to Alec because he wasn't sure how to put into words everything else he was feeling.

"That's good," Alec said.

"Good? How do you figure?"

"I just remember when she took the job in New York and you guys were sort of cooling off, you couldn't wait to go out, remember? She'd barely cleared the city limit sign before you were on the phone to me and we were making plans to go out. This time…it's different," Alec said.

So the inner changes were reflected on the outside…at least to his brother. "It is different. I want more with her, but I'm not sure…"

"You know my track record with women is pretty much three dates and then it all goes to shit, so I can't really offer you any advice," Alec said. "Diego would probably have some."

"Yeah, but I don't want him to give me big brother advice, you know?" Mauricio said.

His brother just clapped a hand on his shoulder. It wasn't that they had some tingly twin sense, but they both just understood each other better than anyone else ever could. Or at least Mo would have said that was true before Hadley. Before this time with her. By letting down his guard, he'd shown her his true self and now she knew him better than anyone else, possibly even Alec.

"What are you going to do about Hadley?"

Mauricio knew he wanted to ask her to marry him, but he was hesitating. He never hesitated. Not about anything. So why now? Did his gut know something his heart and his head didn't?

Was he missing something?

"Seriously, dude, you have to stop making that face," Alec said.

Mo shot his brother the finger. "She makes me…"

"Crazy?"

"Ha. I just want everything to be perfect."

"Honestly, Mo, I think that was the problem with you two the first time. Life isn't perfect, it's messy and it's complicated, and that's what makes it worth living."

"Are you kidding me right now? That sounds like something Bianca would say," Mauricio said as he glanced at his brother.

"She did say it when our sweet nephew painted on my Brooks Brothers jacket. To be fair, it was a picture of him and me on a horse, but it was Brooks Brothers."

Mauricio laughed. His brother might spend most of his time at his computer writing code, analyzing algorithms and making sure his high-end clients' social media presence enhanced their brand and message, but Alec was also a clotheshorse. He always was faultlessly dressed. Not that Mo and his other brothers were rocking the grunge look, but Alec paid special attention to his image.

"I feel ya. So do we think Bianca is right about this? That we should embrace the mess?"

"Yes. I'll deny this if you repeat it, but she's damn smart, probably smarter than any of the rest of us."

"Probably?"

"I was trying to give us the benefit of the doubt."

Mo smiled. "Thanks. How do I apply that to me and Hadley?"

Alec shook his head. "I don't know. But we both have experienced things that were supposed to be perfect or a sure thing that didn't work out. I think with you and Hadley, there's some kind of connection that only works with the two of you. Don't screw it up."

He was trying not to. But he wondered if by focusing on all the things he'd done wrong the last time, he was missing some of the moments he'd gotten right, and that wasn't what he wanted.

He needed to trust his heart and his gut when it came to Hadley. He knew that if he didn't, he'd always be on guard and that wasn't the way to move forward. That was just as bad as pretending to want a relationship the way he had the first time. The scary part was that this time he wanted everything he'd treated so lightly the last time he was with her. It would serve him right if she just wanted to keep being friends with benefits.

But Hadley had never been easy to predict, and it seemed to him that she wasn't the kind of woman who would be satisfied with anything less than a full commitment.

When Zuri and Josie texted her to see if she could hang out, Hadley texted them back that she was in New York. She was surprised that they were together. Josie had been spending pretty much all of her free time with Manu.

Her phone buzzed, and she answered the video call to see both of her friends sitting on the front porch of Zuri's townhouse with glasses of iced tea.

"Why didn't you tell us?" Zuri asked. "We thought you'd be in Houston with Mo."

"I'm sorry. It was a last-minute trip," Hadley said. "I had been planning to go with Mo to the gala though."

"It's okay. We were hoping for some gossip from you about Scarlet O'Malley."

"How would I have gossip about her?" Hadley asked. Scarlet was from a famous—or maybe notorious—family. They had more money than Midas and scandal and tragedy seemed to follow them wherever they went. Scarlet had a reality television show that was in its seventh season. She'd started it the year her sister had died of a drug overdose.

The tabloids were always speculating that she was searching for a father figure, as her normal type was twenty years her senior and into the jet set party lifestyle that was her world.

"She's going to be at the gala tonight," Josie said. "Which I only know because she was linked to Manu last week on TMZ."

Now Hadley remembered. Scarlet was going to hand out one of the awards. According to Mo, it was to show she'd turned over a new leaf. Hadley wasn't too sure about that, but she did know that Scarlet had recently donated a lot of money to a rehab center on the East Coast in her sister's name. So maybe she was trying to change.

"How was Scarlet linked to Manu?" Hadley asked.

"Apparently they were at a fundraiser in the Hamptons together," Josie said. "He invited me to go but the English department isn't as willing to give time off for a trip to the Hamptons as the athletic department is."

"How are things between you two otherwise?"

Hadley asked, noticing that Zuri had turned to watch Josie, as well.

"I think they're good," she said. "I struggle a little with how busy his schedule is, but for the most part we're doing great."

"Good," Zuri said, putting her arm around Josie. "You'll get used to his lifestyle and he'll adjust to yours."

"I hope so," Josie said. "But back to Scarlet O'Malley... According to TMZ, she has to do some serious damage control on her image... There was a viral video of her—"

"Don't tell me. I don't want to know. She's famous because her family is rich. She hasn't done anything worth celebrating."

"I know," Zuri said. "But it's so much fun to watch the train wreck that is her life."

Hadley had to admit it was distracting to watch someone like that, whose entire life seemed like a runaway train. "Anything else happening in Cole's Hill?"

"The Five Families Country Club has a new COO and no one likes her."

"Who is it?"

"Raquel Montez. She wants to get rid of the old smoking room that smells of cigars... You know, the one that all the good old boys hang out in?"

"I do. That room is gross, but the guys all love it. I'm not sure she's going to get the money from the board to do it."

"Apparently she doesn't need full board approval," Josie said.

Hadley continued to chat with her friends, and when she hung up with them thirty minutes later, she realized that she missed Cole's Hill. She'd always wanted to get out of there, get away from the small-town feeling. But now she wanted to go back. She wanted to talk to her mom and Helena, and find out their opinion on the new country club COO. She was becoming that small-town girl she'd always feared she would be and for some reason she was okay with it.

Mauricio texted her a picture of himself in his tuxedo with the caption How do I look? and she felt the sting of tears as she realized how much she loved him. But she wasn't going to text him that.

She wanted to see his face the next time they were together. Make sure that she was 100 percent sure of her feelings.

She simply replied, Gorgeous.

A kissing face emoji flashed on her phone screen, followed by, Miss you.

Miss you too. I'm trying to change my flight to an earlier one.

Good. Text me your details. Want to stay in Houston for a few days when you get back?

Why?

Just figured it'd be nice to have a reunion without the distraction of our families.

Hadley laughed to herself. Their families were huge and could be intrusive without meaning to be.

That sounds perfect.

She put her phone away and fell asleep thinking about how unexpected this second chance with Mauricio was and how happy she was that she'd gotten it. She didn't dwell on the fact that it had come on the heels of a pregnancy scare, but instead saw it as fate stepping in to show her the kind of man that Mauricio had become.

She'd been struggling to leave him in the past and now she acknowledged to herself that it was because she had still been in love with him. She might have been able to get over him if she'd never gone to the Bull Pit that night. Never danced with him until the music had lowered her inhibitions and led her straight into his arms.

But she had.

And for the first time she embraced it. Maybe the drinks and the music had been like a beacon showing her the very thing she'd been afraid to go after: the man of her dreams.

Not a knight in shining armor, but a real man with faults and charms and so many things that made him just right for her.

Fifteen

Mauricio patted his pocket and the ring he'd purchased for Hadley earlier that afternoon. He had made up his mind that he could follow his gut and still not lose control of his temper and his actions. He'd changed. Now he had to start believing it himself. There was no way he'd be able to convince Hadley that he was a new man if he couldn't even convince himself.

He and Alec had room service delivered to his hotel suite. The food had been sort of questionable looking, but he'd eaten it all the same. Alec had left the room to take a call and hadn't had any of the fettucine Alfredo, which Mo was beginning to think was a good thing as his stomach started to feel like shit. He was violently ill in the bathroom, and when he returned to the living room, Alec came over, putting his arm around Mo's shoulders as he staggered into the room.

"You look like crap," Alec said, leading him to the couch and helping him sit down. "What's wrong?"

He shook his head as he swallowed hard, trying to keep from heaving again. "I think the dinner wasn't very good," Mo said. "Get me some antacids and I'll be okay."

Alec squeezed his shoulder and walked over to the kitchen area. Mo tried to swallow again but felt his stomach wasn't having it and he bolted for the bathroom. He felt weak and light-headed when he staggered back into the hallway and found his brother watching him with more than a little bit of concern on his face.

"Lay down, Mo. You're not going anywhere."

"Whatever, bro, I can't miss this gala tonight. It's a really big deal that they recognized our organization, and if I'm not there, it will reflect badly on us."

Alec pushed him toward the bedroom. "I'll go for you."

"You hate this kind of event," Mo said, but he was already toeing off his shoes as he sat down on the edge of the king-sized bed. Alec helped him out of his jacket.

"I do. But I love you, so I'll do this for you. I'm going to have to borrow your tux though. I don't even have a dinner jacket with me."

Mauricio undressed quickly and the ring box fell

out of the pocket of his trousers as he handed them to Alec.

"I guess you figured out what you are going to do about Hadley," Alec said, picking up the box.

"Yeah, I love her, bro. I can't keep pretending that I'm casual about having her in my life. Damn, don't tell anyone that. I wanted her to be the first one I said that to," Mauricio said.

Alec just laughed. "My lips are sealed. Get your ass in bed and get to feeling better so you can tell her when you see her."

Alec finished getting dressed in the tux and then brought Mo a bowl from the kitchen and a damp cloth for his forehead. "Want me to call Mom and ask her to come check on you?"

"Don't do it. I'm not that sick," he said. Their mom tended to be full-on smother-mode when one of them was sick or seemed to need her. "I thought you loved me."

"I do, but you look really bad… We're talking *Walking Dead* shit here."

"I feel like it, but I think if I just lie here, the room will stop spinning and I'll be fine."

Alec put Mauricio's phone on the bed next to him. "Text me if you feel worse. Are you sure you'll be okay?"

"I'm fine, Alec. Thanks for doing this for me," Mo said. "I wrote a speech and it'll be on the teleprompter. Have you used one before?"

"Yes. When I was valedictorian," Alec said.

"Ass. Stop bragging. You only beat my GPA by .025."

"I still beat you," Alec reminded him.

His brother walked out of the bedroom and Mauricio lay in his bed, watching the ceiling spin around, wishing that Hadley were here with him. That stopped him in his tracks. He'd always needed to be strong and at his best in front of her but now he just wanted the comfort of Hadley.

He took his phone and texted her, even though he suspected she might be out to dinner with her friend Merri. Then he stopped. He didn't want to be that kind of guy who was always texting and not letting her enjoy her time with her friends. So he contented himself with a brief emoji text that just had the kissing face.

He drifted off to sleep, dreaming of asking Hadley to marry him. He knew that he needed to not screw it up the way Malcolm had once he'd gotten engaged. And he had a plan. He glanced down and saw he was holding a piece of paper that just said, *Don't screw up.*

That was his plan. He needed a better one than that.

He woke with a start. His phone vibrated in his hand and he opened his eyes to see it was Alec. He'd texted a picture of the award they'd given him.

Congrats, bro. You okay?

Not dead.

Alec responded with a laughing face emoji.

Mo saw that Hadley had also sent him a good-night text, as well as one that congratulated him on his award.

Saw you on the live feed. Your speech was great. Can't wait to see you tomorrow night.

She had seen the speech? Even though she was mistaking Alec for him, the fact that she had watched meant more to him than he knew it should. She hadn't been out with her friend; she'd been tuned in to the awards ceremony. He glanced at the ring on the nightstand and knew that tomorrow he was going to ask her to marry him.

Night, baby. Can't wait to see you too.

He felt better now, so he got up, got dressed and headed down to the bar. Because he always did his best thinking when he was surrounded by people.

Hadley woke up early and showered, knowing she was going home today. For once that wasn't the only thing that added a spring to her step. She'd spent the night thinking of Mo after their last text exchange and she had that feeling of rightness in her gut.

As she braided her hair for ease since she was traveling and put on a bit of light makeup, she glanced out the window of Merri's third floor walk-up. It faced a brick wall of the building next door. She had once thought that she was meant for life in the big city, but she now realized how much she loved the wide-open space of Texas.

And that made her feel better about her decision to stop her freelance work in New York and just concentrate on jobs in Texas. At first she'd thought it was because of everything going on with Mauricio but honestly, she'd just changed. The idea of waking up to this view every morning wasn't one she relished. And as much as she loved the big city amenities, Cole's Hill offered a lot of entertainment.

She packed her carry-on bag and then glanced at the clock. Merri was moving around the apartment and she grabbed her phone to text Mo before she went to talk with her friend and say goodbye.

There were a bunch of news notifications from her app. To be fair, most alerts she received were from TMZ, so when she clicked on this one, she was expecting to see something about one of her favorite celebs. Not a headline about Scarlet O'Malley and her Texas billionaire hookup. She almost dropped the phone when the image finished downloading and she saw that the Texas billionaire was actually her boyfriend, Mauricio Velasquez.

He was kissing Scarlet O'Malley.

Honestly, she couldn't see his face or much of his body but she saw the tux and his arms, his hair.

She tossed her phone onto the bed.

That jackass.

That big, dumb, lying sack of crap.

That... Oh, God. Was it true?

She didn't want to believe it could be, but she'd

seen him in that very tux in a text he'd sent her earlier and it wasn't outside the realm of possibility that he'd…hook up? Really? Just yesterday he'd been talking about getting a place together in New York and then…

Her stomach seized up and she realized that anger was giving way to hurt. She blinked several times to try to keep from crying, but it didn't work. She sank to the floor with the bed against her back, pulled her knees up and put her head against them. She started to really cry as her thoughts spun out of control in her head.

How could I have been so stupid?

What was he thinking?

Why had she let him back into her heart? She'd known he wasn't the settling-down type. She'd known that Mo was too much of a flirt and a partier to ever be alone. But she'd thought he'd changed. She'd believed him when he had shown her how different he was. But maybe she'd been seeing what she wanted to see.

Wasn't that what Helena had said about Malcolm, that she'd missed the signs of him freaking out because she just was so happy that she saw him as settled and contented with the engagement?

Hadley was a fool.

It was bad enough that she'd rushed back to him from New York the last time and found a woman in his bed. This time…everyone was going to see that picture; everyone would know what he had done.

She knew how hard it was to stop loving him, but

pride was going to make it impossible to forgive this. Plus, how many times did she have to see him with another woman before she realized that that was the man he truly was?

There was a knock on the door.

"Hadley, you awake?" Merri called.

"Yes," she said, wiping her nose on the sleeve of her shirt and going to open the door.

"Oh, girl, what's the matter?" Merri asked.

She started talking but even trying to get the words out made her voice shaky.

"Mo is all over the gossip sites this morning. It looks like he hooked up with Scarlet O'Malley last night."

"What? How is that even possible?" Merri asked.

Her friend pulled her own phone from her pocket, but Hadley wasn't paying attention anymore. She needed to stop being so emotional. She needed to have some backbone, because when she got back to Texas, she and Mr. Velasquez were going to have a chat. And then she was going to put that man in her rearview mirror for good.

No more second chances… Hell, this had been his second chance. Hers too, but she'd been wrong. She should have known when they'd had the pregnancy scare that it wasn't a good way to start over.

"I'm sorry, Hadley. Is there anything I can do?" Merri asked.

"No, I'm fine. Besides, you have to get to work. I'm going to catch an Uber to the airport. Maybe I can get on an earlier flight. I want to be back home, so I can end it with him and then—"

She had to stop talking because she was crying again. Merri hugged her close and held her.

"Maybe there's an explanation that we just don't know," Merri said.

Was there?

She picked up the phone, unlocked it and glanced down at the photo once more. How was he going to explain another woman wrapped around him like a cheap suit?

"I don't think so, Merri. But I will give him a chance to explain," she said. She couldn't wait to hear what he had to say. At least this time he couldn't say they were on a break.

The pounding on the door woke him. He sat up and glanced at the door as Alec walked into his bedroom, his hair standing on end, his shirt unfastened.

"I screwed up," Alec said.

"What did you do?" Mo asked as he got out of bed and walked over to his brother.

"I slept with Scarlet," Alec said. "I think the paparazzi that follow her might have gotten a picture or two of us."

"Okay, it's fine. I don't think it will affect your business," Mo said. "That's really more your area than mine but we can handle this."

"No, Mo, you're not understanding me. They don't think I slept with Scarlet, they think you did," Alec said.

Mauricio shook his head. "What? Why would they think that?"

"I was you last night," Alec said.

"Why weren't you just yourself?"

"It was easier to pretend I was you," Alec said. "Of course, now I totally regret it, but at the time it seemed easier than explaining your absence. And I never expected to end up with Scarlet."

"Fuck."

"I know. I'm sorry."

"Dammit," Mo said, grabbing his phone. He dialed Hadley's number but it went straight to voice mail like her phone was off. "This sucks, Alejandro. I can't believe you—"

"I'm sorry."

"Well, Hadley doesn't know that it was you. She's going to think that it's me."

"Maybe she doesn't know."

He sincerely doubted it. "Do you think that's the case?"

"Uh, no. I already saw the alerts on my phone. I don't know what to do. Does it make you look worse to say that you didn't attend a reception in your honor or let the world think—"

"I don't give a flying fuck what the world thinks. It's Hadley whose opinion matters, and right now she thinks I cheated on her. Again."

"I know that. Listen, what if I call her and explain?" Alec said.

"No. You can't do that. I have to talk to her and… Hell, I don't want to have to explain this. She's the woman I want to spend the rest of my life with and I know her. She's not going to be in a listening mood when she sees me. She's probably going to deck me. And rightly so."

"Not rightly so. I'm the one who did this. Let me fix it."

Mauricio couldn't let Alec do anything of the sort. He had to be the one to talk to her. He should have told her last night that he loved her.

He could be worrying for nothing, but given their past, he knew that Hadley wasn't going to just think there was an innocent explanation for those pictures. He didn't blame her. He was already mentally switching his proposal plan to a grovel plan. Maybe she would see him and know immediately that he would never cheat on her. Not now. Not when they had come so far as a couple. But another part of him knew that she was still leery of trusting him and he didn't blame her.

He didn't really blame Alec either. Mo's past behavior was to blame—it had set Hadley and him on this path.

"I have to fix this," Mauricio said. His phone was blowing up with text messages from everyone who knew him. His mom, Malcolm, Helena and Diego.

He sat down on the bed and rubbed the back of his neck. He needed to fix this. With Hadley but also *for* Hadley. Sure, he could tell her that it was Alec and she could believe him, but he didn't want anyone in town to judge her because of this.

He sent a group text to his mom and brother.

It isn't what you think. I will text more later.

Helena was harder to respond to because her texts were a string of curse words and the final message just read, You stink. She loved you.

"Order us something to eat. I'm going to shower and then we're going to figure this out," Mo said to his brother. Alec looked like he was going to try to explain or apologize again but Mauricio didn't want to hear it. He just walked into the bathroom, put his hands on the marble counter next to the sink and bowed his head.

He hoped Hadley was on the plane and hadn't seen the articles, but he suspected she had. He'd seen the story and he wasn't even looking for it. His stomach felt like it had a rock in the bottom of it. Unlike the time Hadley had walked in on Marnie Masters in his bed, he didn't have mock indignity to fall back on now. He knew no matter what the explanation was and despite his innocence, this was going to hurt her.

The last thing he ever wanted to do was to see her hurt, and there was no easy way out of this. He could say he was sick, but he knew there would be friends from Cole's Hill that had seen him in the bar late last night while he'd been making his plan to propose to Hadley. There were so many places where she would be able to pick apart his story.

If he were in her shoes, would he believe his own story? Would he be able to just say, oh, that makes sense?

He knew he wouldn't. He'd lost his cool when she'd kissed Jackson.

Finally he took out his phone and called her number. This time he left a voice mail. He hoped she'd listen to it and it would help her to see his side in this mess. That he'd changed. She mattered to him in ways that he couldn't really explain but that he needed her to believe.

He showered, dressed and then started making calls. Alec looked hung over but was focused on figuring out the best options to fix the PR mess he'd created. Meanwhile, Helena wouldn't take Mo's calls, so he had to resort to using Malcolm as a go-between to try to figure out how to win Hadley back.

Sixteen

She'd always heard that old chestnut about how you can't go home again, but she had never really understood it until now. Until she saw that voice mail notification from Mauricio and realized that somehow he'd become tied to her idea of home.

The tears that she'd done a pretty good job of keeping at bay burned the back of her eyes and she blinked until they disappeared.

She ignored the voice mail, keeping her large-framed dark sunglasses on as she towed her carry-on bag through the Houston airport. Once she was outside, she didn't know what to do. She didn't have a car with her, and an Uber to Cole's Hill would cost the moon. Should she rent a car?

She felt like she was going to cry again but this

time she kept it together. She was stronger than this. Stronger than a broken heart. She knew she needed to get past the sadness to anger if she was going to be able to get over this, but she had no fire in her. Not right now.

Never had she believed that loving someone was a negative thing, even when she and Mo had broken up the last time. She'd seen it as her chance to find herself as a woman and to move on, which she'd done. But now... Well, now she just felt wounded and vulnerable.

And stupid.

And sad.

Damn.

She had to do something.

She'd rent a car, drive home and then figure out when to see Mo. She could just ignore him for a few days if she stayed in Houston, but she wasn't the kind of woman to run away from her problems and she knew it. She'd always been one to face them head on.

And she really wanted to hear what Mo had to say. Her phone pinged, and she glanced down, expecting to see another text from Helena or her friends, but it was from Mo.

Glad you're safely back in Texas. Please call me.

She sat there. Call him? What was he going to say? She'd forgotten they had each turned on the friend finding app on their devices.

She'd never know if she didn't respond to him and she knew it was past time that she did. So, she called him.

He answered on the first ring.

"Thank you," he said.

"Sure. So, what did you want to talk about?" she asked.

"The photo. It wasn't me," he said.

"It looked like you," she said.

"It was Alec."

Alec.

"Why would Alec wear your tux and go to a gala in your honor?" she asked.

"Because I was sick with food poisoning. He's here at the Post Oak Hotel with me. Would you at least allow me to bring you over here, so I can tell you what happened?" he asked.

Just hearing his voice sort of made her want to believe him. It was just like she'd suspected: she was never going to be able to just walk away from him. She wanted him to not be the man in that photo. And Alec and Mo had changed places before, but she'd always been able to tell the two of them apart.

"Okay," she said at last. This wasn't the kind of conversation she wanted to have on the phone. She needed to see his face, because for all his faults, the one thing that Mauricio always had was his honesty. He had never lied to her. Even when she caught him with Marnie.

"Thank you. I've texted the car service and they have someone at the airport. Where are you?" he asked.

She glanced up at the sign over her head and told him, and then felt her tears stirring again. She hated how reasonable and nice he was being. It had been like a knife to her heart when she'd seen that photo, and she didn't know if she would recover from it. Strangely that picture of the kiss hurt worse than walking in and finding another woman in his bed.

She knew it was because this time they'd overcome so much to be together. And it was Alec kissing the woman, not Mo. But in her heart she wasn't as ready to forgive. She realized how afraid of being hurt by him she still was.

Her hand was shaking so she ended the call, because she realized that she couldn't talk to him. Not now and probably never again if she wanted to keep her cool. Because she loved him.

Whatever had been between them when they'd had their old relationship, it hadn't been love. Not like this.

This was something that wasn't going to lessen with time. This was the kind of pain that was like an open wound, and talking to him, hearing him tell her it was Alec, hadn't fixed anything. Because she knew that she had no walls to hide behind. Not anymore. Not where he was concerned.

"Ms. Everton?"

She nodded at the driver who came over to her.

"I'll take your bag," he said, reaching for her suitcase. She let him take it. He opened the door to a Bentley by the curb and she slid into the back seat. She wanted to close her eyes and pretend that she was going to be okay, but she knew that was a lie.

And lying to herself wasn't something she intended to do. She took out her makeup bag, fixed her mascara and then decided to add some eyeliner. She looked so pale that bronzer was in order too. By the time she arrived at the Post Oak, she had a full face of makeup on and felt like at least to the outside world she didn't look like the hot mess she was inside.

The driver opened her door and she climbed out.

"Please check my bag with the valet. I'll get it after my meeting," she said.

He nodded.

She walked into the lobby with no real plan. Maybe she'd text Mo and have him meet her in the lobby and they could talk in the restaurant. She didn't want to go to his room. Didn't want to be alone with him where she'd be able to say all the things that were tumbling around in her head. Things she'd regret later and would burn all her bridges with him.

He didn't bother waiting in the room for Hadley to come to him. He knew that he was on the back foot and needed to take the initiative. He could justify in his head that he was the innocent party, but he'd hurt this woman too many times in the past to sit in his room and wait for her.

The driver texted to alert him that he was pulling up to the hotel and Mo took the elevator down to the lobby. He stood to the side of the entrance and waited.

Hadley walked in with large sunglasses on her face. She pulled them off and scanned the lobby, and when their eyes met, she started blinking.

His heart broke. Right then. There was no need to ask if she was going to forgive him.

How could she?

How could she reconcile herself to being in a relationship with a man she didn't trust? And it was clear to him now that she still didn't trust him. If he were honest, he'd have to say that she probably hadn't forgiven him for hurting her all the times he had in the past.

And he knew that he didn't have the words to convince her that he was a changed man. *Hell.*

Hell and damn.

He walked over to her and she blinked even more rapidly. He knew she was trying to hold back tears, but a few leaked out and started to fall down her cheeks. He didn't care that she was mad at him or about anything but comforting her because she needed it.

He reached for her, but she stepped back, putting her hand up. "Don't. I'll lose it if you touch me."

He hated that, hated that the one thing he felt like he could do had been taken from him. From them.

"Come on. Let's go to my suite and we can talk."

She nodded. He reached out to put his hand on the small of her back but then dropped it before he touched her. He wasn't sure if one innocent touch was going to push past the fragile control she was using to hold herself together.

He used his card to access the concierge level where his suite was located and then led the way down the hall to his room. Alec had left earlier, and the room was empty.

"Can I get you something to eat or drink?"

"No," she said. Her voice had the husky lower timbre it only had when she was biting back tears.

"Let me say again, it wasn't me with that woman."

She nodded. "I know. I believe you, Mo."

He nodded. "So, what's the problem?"

She shrugged, then turned her back to him and walked toward the window. She stood in front of it with her head bent, and he wished he couldn't see her reflection in the glass. Couldn't see that lost look on her face.

"I just realized a few things today. Well, first I thought it was you. And you know that really floored me because what does that say about us as a couple that I thought you couldn't go to one party without hooking up?"

He cleared his throat. "I don't know. Not anything good."

She turned around.

And he wished she hadn't. If he thought she looked lost in the reflection from the window, seeing the expression on her face directly was a thousand times worse.

"Exactly. That photo made me face something that I wasn't aware I was ignoring," she admitted. "I'm not sure I ever really forgave you for anything."

"Fair enough," he said. "But now that we know there's a problem, we can work it out and move past it."

Please, God, let us be able to do that.

She chewed her lower lip and wrapped her arms around her waist, and he knew.

They were never going to be able to move past this.

Fucking hell.

A litany of curses all directed at himself rained through his mind. He'd tried so hard to fix the problems his quick temper and selfish behavior had created. He'd fooled himself into believing that he could fix everything but now he knew. He saw on her face that he was never going to be able to fix the wounds he'd carved so deeply on her soul.

"I guess that's a no."

She shook her head as she started to cry, and he saw her throat work as she swallowed.

"I want to say yes," she said in that voice that made him feel like the worst sort of monster, because he was the one responsible for her hurt and her tears.

"Then say yes. I'm different, Had. You know I am," he said, coming over to her because his arms were starting to ache from not holding her. "I've made huge leaps in the last few months. Losing you showed me all the things about myself that I didn't really like, the stuff I needed to change."

She nodded, and he reached for her. She let him hug her, but she was stiff and the embrace wasn't enough. He didn't know how to get through to her.

She had to at least meet him halfway. Or be open to meeting him.

She rested her forehead on his chest, and he felt

her arms snake around his waist, holding him tightly to her. Then she let her arms drop and stepped back.

"I wish I were a different woman, but I'm not. I don't think I can be what you need because of our past. I wish that we'd waited to get together until now, but we didn't, and I can't forget how you hurt me before. I thought I could. I thought I'd moved past it and forgiven you, but then I woke up to that photo and knew I hadn't.

"This is on me, Mo. The man you are becoming is so much stronger than the guy you used to be, and I wish you nothing but happiness in your life," she said.

Then she moved past him, heading toward the door.

Mauricio knew that if she walked out that door she wasn't going to come back, and he couldn't just let her go. He thought of the ring in his pocket and the plan he'd developed last night in the bar but all of that meant nothing.

"Hadley!"

She stopped but didn't turn around. She just stood there, shoulders bowed, and he knew that whatever he did next was going to be the difference between having her by his side for the rest of his life and living with regret and pain.

"I love you."

The words weren't what he had planned to say but there they were, hanging in the room between the two of them. *Dammit*. He'd never felt so defenseless before. He'd never felt so scared of anything as he was of that she wouldn't respond and just keep walking away.

She turned to face him.

"What did you say?" she asked, but her voice was different now. Not that deep timbre that scraped across his soul and made him feel like he was going to break.

"I love you," he repeated, meeting her eyes and standing up taller.

He was proud of the affection he had for her. She'd made him realize that life wasn't just a race to have the biggest bank account or beat everyone else to the top. That life was sweeter with her in it.

Tipping her head to the side, she asked, "Why?"

"Hell, woman. I don't know why. If I did, then I wouldn't feel like this. I'm a mess thinking that you might leave, and I'll never be whole again. All I know is I love you," he said.

She nodded and then started walking toward him. "I love you too, Mo. I don't know how to stop this. When I saw that picture, I was broken, not angry. There was no anger because you own my heart and my soul, and I didn't want to believe that I could feel that deeply about you and it would mean nothing to you."

"It means everything to me," he said. "I'll do whatever you need me to in order to make this right."

"Loving me is all I need," she said.

"Well, then, we're good, woman, because I love you so damned much," he said, closing the gap between them and lifting her into his arms. She wrapped her legs around his waist and he stared down into her eyes.

He saw the truth of her emotions and knew that they'd have to sort out the photo and how to handle it with the wider world, but the two of them—the people who really mattered—knew the truth and they were together.

He'd never felt so relieved or happy in his life. She wrapped her arms around his shoulders. "I love you so much."

He laughed as joy coursed through his blood. He spun them around in the middle of the suite, holding her to him.

"Me too, darling."

He carried her into the bedroom and set her on her feet. Blood rushed through his veins, pooling in his groin and hardening him as she started unbuttoning his shirt. Her fingers were cool against his skin as she worked her way down his body. When she finished unbuttoning the shirt, she pushed it open and he shrugged out of it.

He growled deep in his throat when she leaned forward to brush kisses against his chest. Her lips were sweet and not shy as she explored his torso. Then he felt the edge of her teeth as she nibbled at his pecs.

He watched her, his eyes narrowing. His pants were feeling damned uncomfortable about now. Her tongue darted out and brushed against his nipple. He angled his hips forward and put his hand on the back of her head, urging her to stay where she was.

"I missed you," she said.

She had one hand braced on his chest as she leaned over him. He shifted under her and lifted her in his arms so that she straddled him. He leaned up and kissed her lips. "I missed you too. I thought I lost you."

"I'm sorry," she said, wrapping her arms around his shoulders and burying her face in his neck. "I can't believe how much I love you."

"Me too."

He tugged at the hem of her blouse, pulling it up over her head and tossing it aside. She was wearing some kind of bralette thing; when he couldn't figure out how to get it off, she laughed, pulling it over her head but not all the way off. Her breasts fell free and he cupped them, rubbing his fingers over her nipples. His cock, which had been hard since she'd jumped in his arms, strained against his trousers.

She shivered in his arms and rocked against him. His cock responded by twitching against her core. He rubbed his hands over the length of her naked back. He enjoyed the feel of Hadley in his arms and it was especially poignant now since he'd almost lost her forever.

She put her hands on his shoulders and eased her way down his chest. She traced each of the muscles of his stomach and then slowly made her way lower. He could feel his heartbeat in his erection and he knew he was going to lose it if he didn't take control.

When she reached the waistband of his pants, she stopped and glanced up into his eyes.

Her hand went to his erection, brushing over his straining length. He reached up and removed the bra she still wore and then lifted her slightly so that her nipples brushed his chest.

She nibbled on her lips as he rotated his shoulders so that his chest rubbed against her breasts.

Blood roared in his ear. He was so hard, so full right now, that he needed to be inside her.

Impatient with her leggings, he lifted her off his lap and tugged them down her legs. She bent over to take them off and he couldn't resist moving around behind her. He caressed her ass and then let his hands move down her thighs. He positioned her so she could lean on the side of the bed. She moaned as he touched her center and then sighed when he brushed his fingertips across the crotch of her panties.

The lace was warm and wet. He slipped one finger under the material and hesitated for a second. She looked over her shoulder at him.

Her eyes were heavy-lidded. He felt the minute movements of her hips as she tried to move his touch where she needed it.

He pushed the fabric of her panties aside and lightly traced the opening of her body. She was warm and wet and so ready for him. It was only the fact that he wanted her to come at least once before he entered her that enabled him to keep his own needs in check.

She shifted against him and he thrust into her with just the tip of one finger. He teased them both with a few short thrusts.

"Mo…" she said, her voice breathless and airy.

"Yes, darling?" he asked, pushing his finger deep inside of her.

Her hips rocked against his finger for a few strokes before she was once again caught on the edge and needing more. He reached for a condom and put it on.

"Take me, Mo."

He pulled his finger from her body and traced it around her clit. She rocked her hips frantically against him. Her hips pushed back toward him and he reached around her to take the tip of one breast in his hand.

He lowered his mouth to the base of her spine and then slowly licked his way up her back, kissing the nape of her neck and biting it. She shuddered in his arms, her hips pushing back against him again. He swiveled his hips and found the opening of her body. She moaned as he brushed the tip of his cock against her humid center.

He scraped his fingernail down her back as he thrust into her. He took her hard and deep, thrusting into her again and again until she called out his name. Then he felt his orgasm rock through him. He drove into her until he was empty and then wrapped his arm around her waist and fell to the bed, drawing her with him.

She curled against his side, her hand moving over his chest as their breath slowed and he looked over at her.

She was his.

Now and forever.

"I have something for you," he said, shifting around to reach for his pants.

"You just gave me something," she said, wriggling her eyebrows at him.

"I'm going to give it to you again after I recover," he said, "But I have something else for you right now."

He took the box out of his pocket and shifted to his side so he could look down into her eyes.

"You know I love you more than life itself, Hadley, and you might need more time. But I want you to be my wife. I want to spend the rest of our lives together. Will you marry me?"

She sat up as he held out the box. He realized he might have planned this better, but if he'd learned anything in his relationship with her, it was that he couldn't wait for perfection. He had to seize the moment when it came along.

He opened the box and took the ring out of it, while he waited for her answer.

"Had?"

"Yes, Mo. Yes, I will marry you. I love you."

He put the ring on her finger and then made love to her again.

Having Hadley in his arms made him realize that all the posturing and fighting he'd done his entire life had been to hide the pain of not feeling complete. He'd been so afraid to let his guard down and let her in but he knew he was better for having her by his side.

Epilogue

Helena and Hadley were waiting outside of the Jaqs Veerland Bridal Studio for their fiancés and Hadley couldn't help smiling at her sister. "I can't believe we're both getting married in the next nine months."

"Me neither," Helena said. "Malcolm is really doing so much better and I'm almost afraid to believe how happy we are at this moment."

"I know what you mean. After that photo of Scarlet and Alec appeared, I wasn't sure that Mo and I would ever be here. But I love him so much, Helena. I never thought I would."

"I know, sweetie. It's hard to believe that we both have found true love."

"Is it?" Hadley asked. "I think we both found what

we were looking for, or at least I did. Mauricio has turned into the man I always knew he could be."

"Well, we were all ready to tar and feather him when that photo showed up online, but once we saw him with you, well, even Mom said there is no way that he could kiss someone else and look at you the way he does."

"Of course, there isn't," Mauricio said, coming up behind them and hugging Hadley. "She owns me body and soul."

* * * * *

*Will there be consequences
for Alec Velasquez's indiscretion?*

Find out in
One Night, Two Secrets

by USA TODAY *bestselling author
Katherine Garbera.*

*Available November 2019
from Harlequin Desire.*

*Emerson Maxfield is the perfect pawn for rancher
Holden McCall's purposes. She's engaged to a man
solely to win her father's approval, and the sheltered
beauty never steps out of line. Until one encounter
changes everything. Now this good girl must marry
Holden to protect her family—or their desire could
spell downfall for them all...*

Read on for a sneak peek at
Rancher's Wild Secret
by New York Times *bestselling author Maisey Yates!*

"I'll tell you what," he said. "I'm going to give you a kiss.
And if afterward you can walk away, then you should."

She blinked. "I don't want to."

"See how you feel after the kiss."

He dropped the ax, and it hit the frozen ground with a
dull thump.

He already knew.

He already knew that he was going to have a hard time
getting his hands off her once they'd been on her. The
way that she appealed to him hit a primitive part of him
he couldn't explain. A part of him that was something
other than civilized.

She took a step toward him, those ridiculous high
heels somehow skimming over the top of the dirt and
rocks. She was soft and elegant, and he was half-dressed

and sweaty from chopping wood, his breath a cloud in the cold air.

She reached out and put her hand on his chest. And it took every last ounce of his willpower not to grab her wrist and pin her palm to him. To hold her against him, make her feel the way his heart was beginning to rage out of control.

He couldn't remember the last time he'd wanted a woman like this.

And he didn't know if it was the touch of the forbidden adding to the thrill, or if it was the fact that she wanted his body and nothing else. Because he could do nothing for Emerson Maxfield, not Holden Brown, the man he was pretending to be. The man who had to depend on the good graces of his employer and lived in a cabin on the property. There was nothing he could do for her.

She didn't even want emotions from him.

But this woman standing in front of him truly wanted only this elemental thing, this spark of heat between them to become a blaze.

And who was he to deny her?

*Will their first kiss lead to something more
than either expected?*

Find out in
Rancher's Wild Secret
by New York Times *bestselling author Maisey Yates.*

*Available November 2019 wherever
Harlequin® Desire books and ebooks are sold.*

Harlequin.com

Want to give in to temptation with
steamy tales of irresistible desire?

Check out **Harlequin® Presents®,
Harlequin® Desire** and
Harlequin® Kimani™ Romance books!

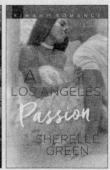

New books available every month!

CONNECT WITH US AT:

Facebook.com/groups/HarlequinConnection

Facebook.com/HarlequinBooks

Twitter.com/HarlequinBooks

Instagram.com/HarlequinBooks

Pinterest.com/HarlequinBooks

ReaderService.com

**ROMANCE WHEN
YOU NEED IT**

PGENRE2018

Love Harlequin romance?

DISCOVER.

Be the first to find out about promotions, news and exclusive content!

 Facebook.com/HarlequinBooks

 Twitter.com/HarlequinBooks

 Instagram.com/HarlequinBooks

 Pinterest.com/HarlequinBooks

ReaderService.com

EXPLORE.

Sign up for the Harlequin e-newsletter and download a free book from any series at **TryHarlequin.com.**

CONNECT.

Join our Harlequin community to share your thoughts and connect with other romance readers!
Facebook.com/groups/HarlequinConnection

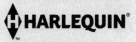

HARLEQUIN®

**ROMANCE WHEN
YOU NEED IT**

HSOCIAL2018